Mayday!

Just then, several hands grabbed our feet and legs and—heave-ho—we were dropped like dead Mafia guys over the side of the bridge. With a half-splash, half-crunch—the melty ice water was only two feet deep at the deepest part—we landed flat on our backs. Under the six-foot-high bridge. Like a couple of trolls.

There definitely were laughing voices trailing off down the road as we stood there mucking off.

High, frivolous, no-rules-type evil laughing voices.

"I wish I had a buck for every time I had this dream," Jerome said calmly, shaking himself off like a dog.

"In yours," I asked, "are there always girls' voices laughing at you in the background?"

"How did you know that?"

"Never mind," I answered, helping him up the bank. "What we need, Jerome, is numbers. Bulk. Men. We need more troops."

#1

JOHNNY CHESTHAIR

Also by Chris Lynch

ICEMAN

SHADOWBOXER

GYPSY DAVEY

SLOT MACHINE

Blue-Eyed Son #1—MICK

Blue-Eyed Son #2—BLOOD RELATIONS

Blue-Eyed Son #3—DOG EAT DOG

POLITICAL TIMBER

He-Man Women Haters Club #2—

BABES IN THE WOODS

JOHNNY CHESTHAIR

Chris Lynch

📖 HarperTrophy®
A Division of HarperCollins*Publishers*

Johnny Chesthair
Copyright © 1997 by Chris Lynch
All rights reserved. No part of this book may be used or reproduced in
any manner whatsoever without written permission except in the case of
brief quotations embodied in critical articles and reviews. Printed in the
United States of America. For information address HarperCollins
Children's Books, a division of HarperCollins Publishers,
10 East 53rd Street, New York, NY 10022.

Library of Congress Cataloging-in-Publication Data
Lynch, Chris.
    Johnny Chesthair / Chris Lynch. — 1st ed.
        p.   cm. — (The He-Man Women Haters Club ; #1)
    Summary: Feeling terrorized by girls, thirteen-year-old Steven and three
of his friends form a club to learn how to become he-men.
    ISBN 0-06-027414-X (lib. bdg.) — ISBN 0-06-440655-5 (pbk.)
    [1. Clubs—Fiction.   2. Sex roles—Fiction.   3. Interpersonal relation-
ships—Fiction.]   I. Title.   II. Series: Lynch, Chris. He-Man Women
Haters Club ; #1.
PZ7.L979739Jo   1997   96-22942
[Fic]—dc20   CIP
                                                                  AC

1   2   3   4   5   6   7   8   9   10
❖
First Edition

Contents

1 The Monica Haunts   1

2 Jerome   4

3 More Troops   20

4 Wolfgang on Wheels   26

5 Is It the Girl, or the Cookies?   40

6 Sinkin' Lincoln and Ling-Ling   43

7 Right All Along   58

8 Johnny Junior   66

9 Captains America   80

10 The High Dive   92

11 What Do You Want, a Badge
   or a Chest to Pin It On?   97

12 All the Rage   113

13 The Coup   127

1

The Monica Haunts

I hate her.

You'd hate her too.

But don't get me wrong, she hates me also.

I hate her so much, I dream about her. If that's not hate, I'd like to know what is.

I've hated her since the third grade, that horror-of-horrors day when the whole class marched in a circle, chanting it. Like devils, all holding hands, and chanting, right there in the schoolyard.

Steven loves Monica, Steven loves Monica, Ste-ven lo-oves Mon-i-ca. . . .

And they had us pinned there, me and what's-her-name, in the center of their vicious circle, where we couldn't escape it.

So of course I hit her. Go on, you would have done the same thing. It was her fault. It had to be her fault. I never would have done anything to get them started on something so stupid. . . . Steven loves . . . it had to be her. So of course I hit her.

So of course, she hit me back.

But see, this is the kind of thing girls just don't understand. There are rules. In this world, there have to be rules so that we can all understand each other. Without those rules, see, nothing makes sense, and we all go around feeling crazy and confused and maybe even afraid—though I personally don't allow myself to do much fearing. For instance, you can't get mad and shoot a guy. Just not cool. I mean, you can do it all right, but then you have to go to jail for it. Makes sense, right, so we don't just all go around popping off on each other every day on the sidewalk. And your parents, they are not allowed to have, like, other families, fathers with fifty wives, you know, none of that. It would just be too confusing, and everybody would be upset, so it's out.

Girls, though. They don't get the rules. Or they don't like the rules. Or they don't care about the rules. Because for whatever reason, girls sure don't *play* by them.

Like when I hit Monica. I hit her on the shoulder, with the meaty part of the fist that runs between the pinky knuckle and the wrist. A non-lethal punch, to say the least. For those civilized among us who play by *the rules* in life, a similar hit would be expected in return.

That's what I expected.

That's what I anticipated as I closed my eyes.

That's right, I said I *closed* my eyes. I have never closed my eyes on a girl since.

I had my first Monica dream right there in the nurse's office as I sat, weaving in and out of consciousness, sniffing the wake-up ammonia, and the nurse interrupting my dream with all that "How many fingers?" and "What day is it, Steven?" business. I could still see Monica's face—white and smooth as yogurt, round, framed by crazy roped hair that was like red seaweed, slanty small eyes—as she puckered up her whole expression in hatred of me.

There are no rules for girls, and that is the problem.

The other problem is the dreams, the Monica Haunts. I still get them five years later. In fact it's even getting *worse* this year, for no good reason. Almost every night, and sometimes during the day, even when she's sitting only two rows away.

2
Jerome

"First, no dames here. Second, no smutty language."

"Why, Steven?" Jerome asked. Jerome was my first recruit, so there was a lot of ground-zero explaining I had to do with Jerome. "And what does that mean anyway, *dames*? What are those?"

That's where we started, okay. Nowhere, is where we started. The *why*s were not the point. The rules were the point. If you don't have rules, you don't have anything. That's what I had to drill into these guys before I could teach them anything else. If you could teach them anything at all, which I don't know.

So I got three words for these boys: Nation of Islam. We ain't black, any of us, and the religion and god and bow-ties business is probably a little more than we want to bite off, but beyond that, the Nation of Islam has got everything. They *know*.

4

Most clubs won't admit it, but these guys have exactly the profile every operation wants: they are tough; they are clean and wear nice clothes; they are scary as all bejesus.

The Muslims get it. The Dallas Cowboys likewise get it. The Green Berets get it. This club, too, is gonna get it.

Because we got rules, junior. Rules is where it's at. Club's got to start with rules, with telling guys what they can and cannot do, because if you can't live with bossing or being bossed, then why even bother clubbing, right?

"Let me tell you a very frightening and devilish story," I said to Jerome back there in the beginning. "There was, way before us, an ultimate cool men's club run by a couple of right thinkers named Spanky and Alfalfa. They had it all—great private headquarters, loyal members like Porky and Buckwheat, and very strict rules to live by. But then one day along came a wicked evil creature, whose purpose in life was to do nothing but break up the mighty bond these men had developed. The creature's name was Darla, and she was powerful. So powerful was she that, in like fifteen minutes, she had Alfalfa *insane* in his devotion to her, betraying his fellow men left and right. Spanky was destroyed, Porky and Buckwheat were confused and left, like, homeless."

"Whoa," Jerome said.

"No kidding, whoa," I answered. "And of course the wicked Darla left Alf chewed like Doublemint and spit, stuck, and trampled on the sidewalk."

"This won't happen to us," Jerome pledged. "No Darlas getting in this club."

"That's right. That's why I tell you this story. That's why we have adopted the name of the late, great He-Man Women Haters Club. So that we do not ever forget."

Jerome pledged he'd never forget.

You may be wondering, Where do you get men for such a club? Let's go back to the start.

First, let's get it right out in the open. I swim, all right? On a team, Speedo suits and bathing caps, and the whole slippery wet picture. And yes, I know what that picture looks like. Ha ha.

I could *play* football, if I wanted to. Or hockey, or baseball, or any other major team sport I felt like. But I don't feel like it.

My father thinks I swim because . . . never mind what he thinks. Let's just say when I was born and he first bounced me—bounced me *wicked* hard, as I recall—on his knee, he was picturing me wearing shoulder pads, not a coating of Vaseline.

It was during fall swim season that I hooked up with Jerome. First, he started showing up at our home meets, which will make a guy stick out in a crowd of four spectators. Then, he became our team manager. Picking up the used Speedos and bathing caps and towels after we were done with them.

Team manager for a junior high swimming team. There's a fairly clear status-snapshot, huh?

I left Jerome pretty much alone. I never jammed my bathing suit over his head when he came by and politely extended the laundry bag. I never grabbed his ankles and pulled him into the pool for a Friday afternoon game of Free Willy/Let's Not. I never stripped him down to his underoos, greased him up, and made him do a bodybuilder posing routine to the music of "The Name Game" (Shirley Shirley bo birley, bo nana fana fo firley, etc.).

But I didn't try to stop all that when it did happen, either. There is a natural order to things, and when you are the swim team manager . . .

Yet even I could witness only so much. The last

day of the season, after the last meet, I was walking home, my hair still wet from the shower and turning to icicles. I was feeling nasty and cheated over my exit talk from the coach.

"You gotta start shaving it, Steven. Or a depilatory cream would be even better."

"This is a joke, right, coach?"

"Look at the other guys. You see any body hair on 'em? It slows you down in the water. You gotta be aerodynamically cutting edge if you're gonna be competitive."

I rubbed my chest absentmindedly.

"I could slick it down, with hair spray or mousse or—"

"Off. Steven, either the hair or yourself, but one of you's gotta be off the team by the spring."

So I was walking in a daze through the slushy street. I wanted to swim, but it had taken me thirteen years to grow those hairs. That's three hairs per year, by my count, and the only way he was getting them off me was with a flamethrower.

I was depressed when I reached Lars's Garage. Lars is my uncle, my father's brother, and he always lets me hang out at his auto restoration shop. He even lets me have my own car, a black 1956 Lincoln that's been sitting in there since 1971.

"You're absolutely right, Steven," Lars said when I told him my dilemma. "Don't you give up them chest hairs to nobody, under no circumstances." He unzipped his one-piece jumpsuit, which was olive green in some spots, motor-oil brown in others, and speckles of a million different paint colors all over. Once he had that open, he popped wide his urban-cowboy denim shirt with the embroidered flowers and pearly purple snaps where the buttons would be on a normal shirt. After that, he pulled up his T-shirt to reveal a tattoo of a snake weaving in and out of his very visible rib cage, and a thin garden of reddish chest hair growing in a patch shaped like a baby's handprint.

"That's your manhood right there," he said, brooming the wisps with his fingertips. "Look at 'em, wouldja? Thirty-nine little oaks."

"Thirty-nine?" I was stunned. "Thirty-nine? Lars, you have thirty-nine? *I* have thirty-nine."

"Course ya do," he said, grinning. "We all do. That's your family legacy. Your old man's got thirty-nine too. All the more reason you gotta look out for 'em. You got your full set right there. They might get a little longer, a little thicker, but you ain't gonna get a single one more as long as you live."

"Jeez," I said, petrified. I mentioned to my uncle that this was the first really big challenge to my manhood I was going to have to face down.

"Ya, the first of about fifty million," Lars said. "So you better get good at it. *Everybody* in this world wants a piece of a guy's manhood."

So we were standing there, the two of us stroking our own sternums, when the banging and cackling started outside. It sounded like fat rain on a tin roof, with witches flying around in it. Lars and I went to the door and cracked it to see.

Nothing this pathetic had ever happened in front of me before. There, scrunched down on his haunches in a corner of the big garage doorway, was Jerome. Across the street from him, fanned out like a squad of snipers, was a group of six girls, winging snowballs at him, pummeling him like an arcade dummy. Their coats were open to the cold—oh, you're *so* tough, girls—exposing their highly decorated Girl Scout uniforms.

I pulled the door shut.

"Whadja do that for?" Lars demanded.

"I think I'm going to barf," I said. The pounding on the garage door increased, like they'd gone semiautomatic. A whimper from Jerome snaked under the door, meaning he'd slunk down to pavement level.

"You can't just leave him out there, Steven. They're wicked. I know those Girl Scouts. They might not leave him alive."

"Ya? Well, I know them too. Know one of them *real* well. In fact, she's their king."

We listened some more. Some of the shots sounded like they could shatter the door, and from the placement of Jerome's moans—holding tight down there at street level—it didn't appear he was going to break away anytime soon. He was pinned, and they were not through with him.

"I suppose," I sighed.

The two of us pulled our shirts back down, and our collars up, and on the count of four blasted out the door. I heard Satan's Scouts squeal when we came into view, and they unloaded on us as we scurried out to retrieve the body. We hung tight, shielding each other just like in the war movies, although we slithered snug to the wall, like rats do.

Jerome was borderline lifeless when we hauled him in, but he was full of life once he realized what we had done.

"Oh my god, thank you thank you thank you," he said.

I stared down at him, lying there flat out on the garage floor. He looked even smaller than I'd thought. He had small bones, little fine hands, a head like a perfect honeydew melon, with thick, short brown hair that looked like he brushed it in circles rather than down or over or back like the rest of us do. His ears stuck out about ten inches on either side of his head.

All I could feel by then was embarrassed. "If you tell anybody I had anything to do with this pathetic scene—"

"You want me to go scare 'em?" Lars butted in. Seemed Lars was taking all this pretty personally now, with his pink face heading for purple. "Rotten Girl Scouts. Always the same, never changes. Jeez, when I was your age . . . Huh, kid, you want me to scare 'em good for ya? So they don't bother you again?"

"This is *really* embarrassing," I said. "Why don't we just cut our losses and—"

"Yes," Jerome blurted.

That was all Lars needed. He jumped to his feet, unzipped and jumped out of his jumpsuit—"Now you know why they call it a jumpsuit," he growled, totally serious—and charged out the door.

"I would have kept the jumpsuit on," Jerome

said to me as we watched the door. "Doesn't that make more sense?"

I shrugged, but I knew my uncle. "He's making a statement . . . or something."

"Hey!" Lars's voice boomed outside. "You. And you. Why don't you all go sell some cookies or somethin'. Don't you come around here and think—"

Lars's message was interrupted by the sound of thunder. Only it was not thunder. It was the sound of six Girl Scouts throwing as many half-frozen snowballs in ten seconds as it is humanly possible to throw. And it was the sound of one auto restorer bouncing off the metal door of his own establishment.

"Where's Stevie?" sang the Haunt. "Doesn't little Stevie want to come out and play?" This was the thing, the whole rotten thing of it how they— okay, how *she*—just can't let it alone. Like Darla, they just *had* to get into *your* castle and muck it all up just in case you were having any fun they didn't know about. "Come out, come out, Stevie," Monica hooted.

Jerome and I were dead silent when Lars staggered back in. He tried to keep it together, dusting snow and ice chips off himself calmly. The

13

embroidery on his shirt now looked like it was the Alps instead of flowers. He picked up his jumpsuit and dragged it toward his office, like Linus with his blanket.

"I forgot," he said. "I'm not supposed to do that. With the probation . . . I ain't allowed to do no scarin' people off. Sorry, kid."

I shook my head sadly. "Girls," I growled.

"Well," Jerome offered, "*these* girls, anyway. Maybe they're not all like that."

"Yes they *are*," Lars snapped before he slammed the door to his office.

Jerome finally got to his feet. "You're on the swim team," he said.

"Maybe," I answered. "What's it to ya?"

I don't make friends easily.

"Sure you are. I'm the manager. Cut it out, you know me."

I shrugged. "Ya, I do know you, but no, I might not be back on the team. They're asking for compromises I'm not prepared to make."

"Really?" Jerome sounded interested. "What kind of compromises?"

I looked him up and down. Shook my head. "Forget it. You wouldn't understand."

I walked away from the kid, and got right into

my Lincoln. I sat, like always, in the driver's seat, adjusted my rearview. Good, he was gone. Adjusted my sideview. Bad, he was not gone.

"So what do you do here? I mean, what *are* you doing here? Do you work here? Whose car is this? It's a great car. You hang around here all the time? Is that all right? Can anybody just . . ."

He was like talk radio. I turned away from him, pretended to be tooling down the highway while Jerome chattered on. I turned the volume knob down, beeped the dying-moan horn twenty times. He didn't seem to notice.

"It's my uncle's place," I said finally. "That was my uncle. And *this*"—I tapped the Lincoln's dashboard with my index finger—"is mine."

"Holy *smokes*," Jerome said, jumping back. "This whole thing is *yours*? That's unbelievable. I mean . . . unbelievable."

I watched as Jerome crouched down and looked at his reflection in the chrome full-moon hubcaps. Polishing was my specialty.

"Unbelievable. I mean, I believe you, but this is just . . . immense, a kid owning a thing like this."

Jerome got it. Some people don't get it. But Jerome *got* it.

"Go on," I said, pointing across the broad front

bench seat toward the passenger door. "You can ride shotgun."

He raced, and slammed the door before I could tell him . . .

"*Don't* slam the doors, Jerome. It needs work. The doors can fall off, you know."

"Won't do it again, Steven. All right I call you Steven?"

"Sure, what else you gonna call me?" I turned away from him and considered the road again, with the steering wheel in my grip. "See, Lars gave me this car because he thinks I can't get into trouble with it, because it's been here for twenty-five years and nobody can fix it. *Ha.* Little does he know I plan on getting into *big* trouble with it. He lets me keep the battery charged so I can play the radio and flip the wipers and all that kid goo-goo, but that battery is going to *crank* this baby someday. And he can't take it back then. It's mine."

"Wow" was all Jerome could say. I had to turn to give him a look, to find out if he was for real, or if he was zooming me. He was for real. Every idea I had, he was wowing all over it.

"Do you need any help? Like, an assistant or something?"

I thought about it. "No."

Seemed like he was going to cry after that. But he didn't, thank god, because I would have had to get physical with him if he did. But also, he didn't seem to register what I said, because he started showing up at Lars's every day even though I never invited him and we can safely assume that Lars didn't either. He didn't bother me, much, so I didn't kick him out.

"This is probably about the best clubhouse a guy ever had," Jerome piped one day. He'd been coming for two weeks by then and, being a bright kid, had probably noticed that we were doing a lot more hanging around than auto restoration.

This was actually the first time the idea of the Club ever came up. "What clubhouse?" I said. "This is an automobile. It ain't no club."

"Sorry," he said. "It's just that, well, it doesn't move, and I think the 'mobile' part of automobile means—"

"Don't *make* me come over there, Jerome," I said, even though "over there" was only the width of the car's hood.

Jerome clammed up. Which was sneaky. This is the thing with Jerome, the way you tell him not to come over and he shows up anyway and you

17

let him; and you tell him this is not a club and he shuts up like he believes you but really he's just waiting for you to sort of start thinking more like he's thinking. I don't know how he does that.

"So, if it was a club," I said, in my large leadership voice, "what would be the point?"

"Well . . . ah . . . we could hang out. Guys like us, you know, like, individuals, *guys,* who don't belong to any other clubs or anything. Guys who go their own way, who aren't like anybody else. But at the same time, guys who might want, or need, to have a crew of guys like themselves. To back them up, to . . ."

"To be *bigger* than just one guy alone," I joined in. I had to admit, he had me thinking. And he knew he had me thinking, because then he came in for the kill.

"Guys like *me,*" Jerome gushed, "who want to be like *you!*"

Sometimes you can hear something like that, that sounds so plainly like a crock.

And then, a crock doesn't sound so bad.

"Like me?" I bit. "Like, what do you mean, like me? Like what?"

"Like . . . I don't know, like a kind of a guy, like a real guy, like . . ."

"Like a Johnny Chesthair kind of a guy," I was happy to offer.

"Yes!" Jerome said. "Exactly."

So I bought in. Maybe it wouldn't be too bad to hang out with a lot of guys who thought and acted like me. Men with a common goal, and a noble purpose.

And who would do whatever I told them to.

3
More Troops

"I quit," Jerome said for the fiftieth time.

"I'm not chasing you anymore, Jerome," I said for the fiftieth time. "You want to go, go."

He went. I waited. I heard the door shut. I went after him for the fiftieth time.

"What's the problem now?" I asked as we walked our regular, Jerome's-quitting route. Down the parkway, through the glacier hole, alongside the pond where the winter ice was finally breaking up, and down to the arched stone bridge that crossed the nearly dry river.

"I need to *do* something. This club is dead . . . all we do is lie around."

"See, Jerome, that's where you're such a rookie. We're not lying around . . . we're hanging out. That's a very club thing to do. There's really a lot going on beneath the surface when we're there, together, hanging out. Important stuff."

"I want more, Steven. I need more. More man stuff."

Jerome and I assumed thinking position—draped over the cold stone wall of the bridge, heads over the side and aimed down at the riverbed below, making our heads spin with stalled blood.

"Want to kill somebody?" I asked, to lighten the mood.

"No, I'm serious. You have your car, which is great, and your thirty-nine chest hairs and every-thing . . . you're a complete, total *guy*."

Well, I certainly wasn't going to contradict him.

"Total," he said.

"Total," I said.

"Total," Jerome added. The upside-down blood thing makes us a little slow. "But I need something else. Steven . . ." Here he got all very serious on me, which I don't much like but is pretty hard to avoid with Jerome. "I mean this, I need help. You understand me? I *need* more. I need to get more man stuff in me or out of me, or however it works. That's what I got into this club for. You've been given a gift, Steven—the ability to get the most immense pleasure out of the stupidest little rituals. Share that gift with me.

21

"Teach me to be a real guy, Steven. I'm desperate. I don't know how—all right?—and I'm worried about myself."

I looked at him, the two of us hanging there like a couple of exhausted bats. He stared right into my brain, so I looked away. Can't have another guy seeing into your brain. Especially one who's worried about himself.

"What's the manliest thing?" Jerome asked.

"Sorry, man. This is a no-girls club. I told you. . . ."

"What's the next manliest thing?"

"Guns."

"Hmmmm?" Jerome said, apparently thinking that one over seriously.

"Let me interrupt before you get too out of hand," I said. "First is having the gun, but then the big manly thing is, you have to use it. Starting with bottles and cans, I suppose, then little animals, then big animals, then . . . people. If you want to get full, badder-than-the-next-guy man points, you gotta eventually put the gun to work."

"Oh." He seemed to be slowing down, but the idea was still not quite dead.

"Okay, Jerome, so then, assuming you have killed a guy—a big, mean guy, somebody from downtown, let's say, and who was probably pretty close to splattering *your* brains first—"

"I don't like this story anymore."

"Shaddup. Let's say you achieved all that and in the end you award yourself the thirty-nine-hairs medal of honor. You know what happens then? They put you in jail, and in there . . . from what I understand, the whole manliness process gets turned completely around all over again."

Jerome's face went from upside-down-blood red to greenish-purplish.

"Fine," he sighed. "What's the next manliest thing?"

"Easy. Football."

"Forget it, I'd rather do the gun-and-jail thing. But I think you have something there. Sports. That's what I need. Steven, you're an athlete, you know. Help me. Help me get into a sport. What should I do? How do I start? What will it do for me? This is it, right? This is the solution. I will *make* myself be a . . . sports . . . type . . . person."

"Ah, ya. Right," I answered, trying not to sound the way I felt. How I felt was, he might as well have asked, Steven, please go back to the garage and build me a spacecraft so I can link up with the *Star Trek* gang by the weekend, okay?

"Well, ah, Jerome, um, what sports do you *like*, for starters?"

"None of 'em!" he said proudly. "But that's not the point. I'm on a mission. I have no need to enjoy it."

"Oh. Well, that's good," I said. "That's helpful. I think we can come up with something you won't enjoy."

He slapped his hands together loudly, like dinner was being served right there over the side of the bridge.

"But let me sleep on this," I said. "I need to give it some . . ." I stopped. "Jerome, did you hear something?"

Jerome was preoccupied, swiping at the air below, and punching his little fists on the stone of the bridge. As if we had decided on boxing as the life for him. *Not*.

"I think I heard someth—"

I'll be darned if I wasn't right about that. For, just then, several hands grabbed our feet and legs and—heave-ho—we were dropped like dead Mafia guys over the side of the bridge. With a half-splash, half-crunch—the melty ice water was only two feet deep at the deepest part—we landed flat on our backs. Under the six-foot-high bridge. Like a couple of trolls.

24

There definitely were laughing voices trailing off down the road as we stood there mucking off.

High, frivolous, no-rules-type evil laughing voices.

"I wish I had a buck for every time I had this dream," Jerome said calmly, shaking himself off like a dog.

"In yours," I asked, "are there always girls' voices laughing at you in the background?"

"How did you know that?"

"Never mind," I answered, helping him up the bank. "What we need, Jerome, is numbers. Bulk. Men. We need more troops."

4
Wolfgang on Wheels

"Sing me a Christmas song."

"I don't know any Christmas songs, Dad."

"Don't be stupid. Everybody knows at least ten Christmas songs. Sing me a Christmas song, Swimmer."

Swimmer was his nickname for me. It was not a compliment.

"Okay, I do, I know exactly two Christmas songs. Do you want to hear 'Jingle Bell Rock' or 'Happy Happy, Joy Joy' by Ren and Stimpy?"

The old man was stumped. "I never heard of that one. Sounds nice. Do the happy joy one."

Hah. He went for it. So, with all my might, I tore into the song. "*Happy happy, joy joy, happy happy, joy joy . . .*" I screeched, and after I'd sung all *two* of the lyrics thirty thousand times, he got up from the breakfast table, smacked me on the back of the head, and headed out the back door.

He did that a lot, the smacking. Not abusive stuff. I wouldn't ever try and say I was an abused kid. I read *Globe Santa*, about the six brothers under the age of twelve who got punched around by eight different fathers and only wanted one G.I. Joe doll to share for Christmas, so I know what's a bad-news life and what's not. So I know mine's not, and that's why you'll never catch me belly-aching about my life. No, sir, you won't hear me bellyaching.

He'd really bop me, if he caught me bellyaching.

The cuffing from my old man is just communi-cation anyway, not abuse. *Communication*, not abuse. He's just reminding me who's boss, who calls the shots, who's the man, and how that gets decided.

As if I couldn't figure it out without the cuffings.

But enough about me. We're not here to talk about me. We're here to talk about the club.

Jerome had been out scouting since we got dumped in the river by our rivals. He was all excited about this one guy who lived halfway across town, in an area where I didn't even think they *had* houses, just hospitals and warehouses and fingernail salons. A cold and rough part of town.

"Jerome, where are you taking me?"

27

"I told you. To meet somebody. Somebody for the club. He's somebody who could really use you. As a matter of fact, he reminds me a lot of you."

"Cool, then, I like him. But if he reminds you of me, why does he need to learn to *be* like me?"

"He's got . . . some weaknesses."

"Weaknesses."

"Weaknesses."

"What's Mr. Weakness's name?"

"His name . . . is Wolfie."

"Wolfie. He reminds you of me, and his name is Wolfie? How do you know Wolfie?"

"We were in frrdemurfurferapee together." His voice trailed badly toward the end there.

"What? You were in what?"

He got very calm, pronounced his words softly and clearly. The kind of thing you can only do when you're trying really hard.

"Therapy. We were in a group therapy thing together. It was something the schools organized to get boys who couldn't—"

I held up my hands. "I don't want to know. I don't want to know what you couldn't do, Jerome, okay? This here, this He-Man, Johnny Chesthair Club . . . this is going to have to be, like, anti-therapy, because I can't be hearing anybody's *stuff,* okay? Our rule is going to be: You got a problem? Get over it."

"I'm over it," Jerome said grimly.

"Good. So that's settled forever. What's Wolfie's real name?"

"Far as I know, it's Wolfie."

I thought about the possibilities as we approached the cold brick box of a building. The possibilities seemed bleak.

"We're going to have to collect dues in this club, I think. I'm going to need to get paid for this job."

He wasn't listening; he was marching. I followed along as Jerome stepped lively up the ramp that zigged back and forth and back up toward the front entrance of the official, public-looking building that had no name. He pushed through the glass entrance and walked up to the tall, severe lady at the tall front desk.

"Jail, Jerome? You're taking me to meet a juvie jail kid? To join our fine, clean, *American* organization?"

Ignoring me, Jerome inquired at the desk.

"He's not here now," the woman said.

"Okay. Where is he, then?"

"He is allowed to come and go as he pleases . . . within reason."

We both waited on that, since she sounded like she was going to finish up with an actual answer to Jerome's question. But no, that was it.

"So, lady," I blurted, shouldering Jerome out of the way. "Where did Wolfie boy come and go to this morning?"

She looked to me like a famous wicked woman, but I couldn't place her. Her hands were long and spidery; her gray-blond hair was long and spidery. I imagined her legs back there were long and spidery too, as she stretched herself up even taller and looked way, way down on me.

"So what?" I said. "So you're taller than me."

I thought I must have looked pretty imposing right then, feeling my scowl bring her down to my size. But instead of withering, she brought her hand to her mouth, and laughed. At me, apparently.

Tittering, is what you would call it. Stuff only women do. I hate it when they do that. Why do they do that to me?

"I believe he's at the V.R.," she answered finally.

When we were outside, I tried bringing Jerome up to speed, filling him in on the wickedness. He didn't get it, though.

"Really? I thought she was kind of helpful," he

said. "I guess I must've missed the part where she was nasty."

"Jeez, Jerome, you are such a rookie," I said.

The V.R. was a place mostly older, techno-nerdy types hung out, but for the few younger guys who paid attention, it was the graphic leap for when regular video games didn't flick your Bic anymore. The place was actually called "Virtual Life and Death," and specialized in team assaults, space explorations, and BattleTechs into oblivion that you couldn't even play if five other guys didn't want to play with you. They had these maze hallways, private cubbies, posters and video screens and gear hanging off the walls, all tied in to the latest, up-to-the-nanosecond, blow-out-the-eyeballs versions of Virtual Reality thrill kill. And they had a really nice lounge area.

That's where we found Wolfie.

"Wolf*gang* is my name," he howled at me, like an actual wolf-boy.

"Sorry," Jerome said. "I've been calling you Wolfie all this time, so I told Steven—"

"*You* can call me Wolfie," he said to Jerome. "But *you* call me Wolfgang."

"Fine," I said, struggling to remain cool. "Fine, then I'll just—"

"Wolf*bang,* instead."

"Huh?"

"Wolf*bang*. I like the sound of that better. Just made it up. It fits me better, I think. Wolf*bang*!"

I turned slightly to grab a look at Jerome's face. Jerome was smiling, very friendly, at this mean and loud kid. Jerome, it seemed, could like anybody.

"You got a club, huh? I hear you got a club?" Wolfbang asked. "And you came to beg me to be in it."

I looked at Jerome again. He would not look at me, and would not remove the smile. First chance I got, *I* was gonna remove that smile, boy. . . .

"What are you looking at him for?" Wolfbang demanded. "I'm the guy who asked you the question."

"Oh," I said, startled. "Sorry."

Who was this fool? Who was this measly-weasly chump? These were the questions running through my head, but I was asking them not about Wolfwhatever, I was asking them about Steven. Why was I taking this crap from him?

Maybe it was the wheels. He was on wheels. Big wheels. Wheelchair wheels. Wolfgang on Wheels.

So the long black hair slicked and combed straight back, swept-back ears, and Vulcan V-shaped facial features, which made him look like he was always speeding past on a train with his head hanging out the window, didn't even matter a whole lot.

"Keep it down, please," the lounge keeper said. He was serving juice drinks and high-energy snacks from behind the counter. The style of the place was like a hunting lodge, warm and full of wood, only with video monitors strobing away where the animal heads would be mounted.

"And if you're finished playing and you're not buying anything, perhaps you should be moving along."

"Hey," Wolfbang snarled. "If I had the quarter, I'd be playing."

"Get outta here, ya little con artist," the man sneered. "You probably ain't even a for-real crip."

"Let me play on credit, or I'll go out and start begging right in front of your store."

"You little . . ."

This was getting awfully embarrassing. I pulled out the two quarters I had in my pocket and handed them to the kid.

He looked at the quarters in his palm, then up at me. "What do you want me to do with this, feed your parking meter for ya?"

"Hey," I said. "I thought—"

"*Quarter* was just an expression. You wanna play in here, cost ya a fin." He bounced one of the quarters off my forehead. Kept the other one.

"Five *dollars*?" I gasped.

Wolfbang smiled at me, palm extended.

"Well, I don't feel *that* bad," I said, and bolted out the door. As soon as I was outside, Jerome caught up to me.

"You just don't know him yet," he said. "You're really going to get to like him."

"He reminds you of me, Jerome? *He* reminds you of *me*?"

"Well," Jerome said, "he really, really likes cars, and . . . he claims he hates girls . . . well, hates pretty much everybody, but . . ."

The two of us were walking quickly down the sidewalk when the V.R. manager called to us from the front door half a block away. "Hey, you forgot something." As we turned back to look, the man revved up and gave Wolfie on Wheels a mighty shove.

The kid was actually grinning as he tooled down the street at about sixty miles per hour. It took everything Jerome and I had to stop him when he reached us, since he made no effort to slow himself down.

"First off," Wolf said, "is this club handicap accessible? Second, what's in it for me? Is there anything special about you that I should want to join up? And about the name, He-Man Women Haters Club, is that literally, like we have to go out and actively hate 'em, or just kind of a philosophical hate?"

The thing about Wolfbang is, because of who he was, and because of who I wasn't, I couldn't handle him like I should have. I kept looking to Jerome like Wolfbang spoke some screwy foreign language and I needed an interpreter.

"Maybe if you got one of those chairs with a motor," Jerome said. "Maybe then he couldn't shove you like that."

"I got one," Wolfbang said, "but I like to be pushed."

I didn't even wait to be told. I circled back and started pushing Wolf on Wheels toward Lars's Garage.

I couldn't even believe myself. What a dink.

"That's the boy," he said smugly.

That's what I needed. I smacked him across the back of the head.

The Wolf howled; Jerome gasped. Order was restored. I felt better.

For a few minutes.

"So, what, do you guys get some kind of government funding for having handicapped membership, is that what you wanted me for?"

He was like that the whole way back to the garage.

"I'm not cut out for this, Jerome," I whispered after I'd pushed the Wolf a few yards ahead of us. "This whole handicap thing. I don't think I can deal—"

"Hey, it's my legs that don't work, the ears are fine. I can hear you back there."

"So what," I yelled, exasperated. "So you can hear me. So are you mad now? Are you offended, or what? Y'know, Wolfie, if I were you, I'd peel right on out of here. You don't have to put up with this kind of—"

He spun on me, slick, getting his two little front wheels up in the air and holding them there, a wheelie, for several seconds. Then he slowly cruised toward me and we faced each other there on the sidewalk, OK Corral–style.

"I don't think I could be in this weenie club anyway, with you being the boss. You are *so* afraid of me it's funny. I think I might laugh, even."

I turned to Jerome, and pointed at Wolf. "This

is what I'm talking about. This guy needs disciplining. I mean, he *needs* it, but how am I supposed to give him the beating he deserves with—"

He ran into the side of my leg with the sharp metal foot plate on the front of the chair.

"Oww!" I yelled. "That does it. Go on home, ya little freak."

He reached up—somehow his arms could stretch way higher than you'd think—and grabbed me by the collar of my jacket. Before I could react I was down on the sidewalk, down *hard,* and thrashing around with him. It was like a nightmare I couldn't have dreamed because it never would have occurred to me.

"This is so embarrassing," I said, talking even as we wrestled. The two of us were locked together and rolling, like the guys who wrestle alligators, rolling over and over and over until we plunked into the gutter, neither one of us on the top, neither one of us on the bottom.

"Jerr*oooome,*" I called, Wolf's fist pressing into my throat, squeezing my voice into something clownish.

"Don't cry to Jerome," Wolf answered, in the same voice, for the same reason. "You want me off, you get me off."

"All right then, *Wolfie,* I don't want to get tough with someone like you, but I'll do it to get you out of here."

"Hah" was all he had to say.

I went to work. But nothing much happened. First I tried squeezing his neck, but it tightened, even thickened in my hands. I rolled him over, worked him into a headlock. He pulled out of it like a turtle sucking into its shell. When he was behind me, he sank a kidney punch.

"Oh boy," I huffed. "You're in deep now." I was on my knees, and stayed there, I guess because my opponent was sitting. Jerome had drifted twenty feet down the sidewalk, pretending not to know us.

I locked the Wolf into my patented bear hug. He locked me likewise in his.

It would make sense that guys with no use of their legs would develop pretty good upper body strength. But you never really know until you're squeezed by one.

First my breathing got very shallow. Then I saw those spots like when a camera flash goes off right in your face.

Then I woke up. I looked over to see Jerome trying to help Wolf into his chair, Wolf slapping Jerome's bony hand away, then swinging himself up into the chair.

"This is so embarrassing," I said again.

"Hah," Wolf said again.

I sat upright. Stayed there for a few seconds. "Fine, Wolf*bang*," I said. "But it's still my club. Got it?"

"You're the head weenie," he laughed.

"Cool," Jerome said. I had to look closely at him to figure out whether he did honestly think it was, cool. He did.

When Jerome and I walked in the door to the garage, Lars was waiting for us just inside. There was a short step up to get inside the entrance, so I punched the button to lift the electric garage door so that Wolf could get in. Lars stepped back and shook his head as the new member rolled up.

"*Another* one," he said, shaking his head. "What are you doin', neph, raiding the dumpster outside every other club?"

5

Is It the Girl, or the Cookies?

This is one of the Haunts. Comes back all the time. In this dream, Monica is in her Girl Scout uniform, and she's selling cookies. Only she's not like herself, she's about eight feet tall. Behind her, lined up like a basketball team, are her friends, also Girl Scouts, also giants.

"You want a cookie, Steven?" Monica says to me. She's smiling, but I know better. She's smiling at me the way a mean dog smiles when you walk too close to his fence.

Fact is, I would love a cookie, in the dream. But I don't want to tell her, because I'm afraid there's a catch and I'm going to wind up looking like a dope in front of her gigantic wicked Girl Scout friends. So I say no way, I hate Girl Scout cookies, everybody knows that.

40

"Are you *sure*?" Monica coos. "I have somoas here, Steven. I have the legendary chocolate mints, and I have tagalongs."

Holy Smokes, the tagalongs. How can a guy be expected to resist the tagalongs? And free? Free tagalongs? It is never clearly stated, but it is definitely implied that I will not have to pay for these tagalongs. The box is already open, so, sure, they have to be free.

Am I not merely human? A simple man.

I reach for the cookie.

She grows. Like Stretch Armstrong. She holds the cookie between two fingers, holds it out to me, and then shoots up into the sky like a human cherry picker. I jump—because, of course, now I want that tagalong more than I want air.

But, of course, I won't be reaching *that* tagalong anytime soon.

"These cost *money*, you know," she scolds me, while her friends laugh and yell things at me. "Selling cookies is the only way we can finance all the wonderful programs administered by the Girl Scouts of America, providing healthy and rewarding alternatives to today's young women. . . ." Blah blah blah.

You would think I'd get the message. You'd be mistaken.

"So," I say, "do I get the cookie?"

"You do not get the cookie. Buy your own box, ya grub."

"Fine," I say—and this is where I realize it's a dream, because I reach into my pocket and pull out a ten-dollar bill.

Monica snags the money, looks into her bag, looks back at me.

"Sorry," she says. "We don't have any more tagalongs. All that's left are the shortbreads."

And that's where I spring up in bed, sweating. The crappy shortbreads, can you believe it? What a Haunt. What a foul evil thing. Takes me hours to get back to sleep.

The nerve of her anyway, showing up in my dream, puffing herself up so much huger than me. When really she's only two inches taller than me.

Two and a half, max.

6
Sinkin' Lincoln and Ling-Ling

Wolfbang, Jerome, and myself were just opening up for another promising day at the office, when Lars stopped us at the gate.

"I don't know how you do it," my uncle said in a tone of no-admiration. "I don't know how, but you found another one, didn't ya?"

"Another what?" I asked.

"Another I-don't-know-what," he answered, "but there's one more waiting for you back at the Lincoln. Says he's here to join up. 'Join up to what?' I says. 'Join up to the He-Man's World,' or Boys' Room, or Pajama Party, or some such whatever, he says." Lars took a long look around at the crew, staring particularly hard at Wolf, then even harder at little Jerome.

The three official He-Man Women Haters Club members headed toward the rear of the shop to meet the guy who wanted to be number four. And there he was. Whatever he was.

"He's here to join up? Jerome," I growled, "where are you getting these people? You placing ads? You building them in your basement? What?"

"Hmmm. Ummm . . . I think maybe I remember posting just a little thing on the Internet . . . maybe."

"Arrrggghhh!" Wolf and I howled at the same time, our first agreement. "Computer fruiters!"

"Cut it out, you guys," Jerome protested. The new kid just sat motionless on the Lincoln's trunk.

"You never told me you were one of those, Jerome. This could constitute a breach of your club application. This is serious; I'm gonna have to rethink this whole thing now."

"Ya," Wolfbang chimed.

"Ya, Wolfbang and I are going to have to reconsider your application now to be in the He-Man's club."

"You and *Wolfbang*? I'm the one who brought him in."

"Ya," Wolf said. "But I didn't even know you were one of them. If I knew, I would have figured this was one of *them* clubs, and I wouldn't have joined anyhow."

"Ya, no kidding, Jerome," I said. "It is very

important that people don't get the idea that we're the wrong kind of club. We don't want to be known for that."

"For *what*?" Jerome hollered.

It's a hard thing to define, exactly. I struggled. "For . . . you know what I mean."

"For the wrong stuff," Wolf added.

"Exactly. That's what I mean. Wrongness is what we don't want to be known for."

Jerome put his fists—which were actually like two fingers curled up into mini-fists—on his hips. He pulled down a face like nothing I'd seen on him yet, a face like anger. He went all red, his lips tightened, then spluttered as the voice came welling up from his abs.

"Mmmmmmmmorons!" he yelled. He turned and stomped toward the exit.

I shrugged at Wolf, and he shrugged at me. Like we cared, right? We had new business to attend to. Wolf wheeled, and I stepped, a few feet closer to the new recruit. I was opening my mouth to begin the questioning when I heard the door slam. The same door through which we had first dragged the pummeled and frozen Jerome, back at the very birth of the HMWHC.

The noise from the slam echoed through the

45

spacious garage even after Lars yelled out, "Hey, don't nobody slam my doors!"

So, then, what? I stared at the new kid and I felt it gone already. What club? You could practically hear the crickets chirping, it was so dead in there. Rotten Jerome. He sucked the clubness right out the door with him.

"What are you doing?" Wolf yelled as I ran toward the exit. "We got business. Serious business to attend to."

"Be right back," I yelled as I flew out.

"Don't nobody slam my doors!" I heard from just the other side of the metal garage entrance.

"Come back inside, Jerome."

Jerome kept right on stomping, making me follow and . . . sort of, not exactly, but something like, plead with him.

"Come back in, Jerome."

"Get away from me, Steven. I'm going to join a computer fruiters club."

"Hey, you'll hate yourself, man. I mean it. I'm just trying to save you here."

"Don't save me."

I stopped following. I watched him walk down the sidewalk quickly, then a little more slowly, then slower. He tipped a look back over his shoulder, noticed I'd quit chasing, and stopped.

"So, why should I?" he demanded, assuming his favorite fists-on-the-hips stance. "Huh, Steven? Why should I come back to a club where I'm a geek?"

So, I had him. He *wanted* me to chase him. And he wanted to be begged. It wasn't like he was turning down offers from a million other clubs.

"No reason," I said. "You're right, never mind." I started back toward the club.

"Hey," he called, starting after me. "Hey, hey you." He caught up, started tapping me on the shoulder, but I kept on walking. "No, you were saying something back there. About how I should be coming back because you needed me—"

"Dream on, backwash."

"You did, Steven, you said it. And it's because you need somebody smart around because between you and Wolfie you combine for just about enough brains to run a hamster wheel."

My legs are longer than his, so as I picked up my pace he had to jog along to keep up. Very satisfying for me. "Well then, why don't you and your big old computer geek brain just go back to quitting the club, like you were trying to do."

"Until you begged me to come back."

"You been sitting too close to the screen, cyber-boy."

We crossed through the doorway into Lars's without interrupting our debate.

"Oh ya, well, if you weren't bringing me back, what were you doing behind me all that way down the street?"

"I was chasing you *away,* is what."

"Hah, and you couldn't even do *that,* could ya?" Jerome said as he took off his jacket and hung it on the nail right beside the life-size Snap-On Tools Girl poster.

"Ahhh . . ." I ran aground. I not only ran out of things to say, I lost track of what I was trying to accomplish in the first place. Jerome was smart enough to notice.

"And what about my sports idea, huh? You were going to help me get started with the sports thing, remember?"

"Oh, ya." I was in full backpedal now. "I've been thinking about some things. I want to come up with just the right . . . really soon, Jerome, I promise." I wondered how long I'd be able to dodge this one. Truth, of course, was that there was no sport that would boost Jerome's He-Man rating. He had a hockey player's grit, tamped down into a chess-club body. "Hey," I said abruptly. "Let's not be rude. We're ignoring our guest."

Smooth, no?

"He's *in*," Wolfbang crowed, sitting beside the new guy, the two of them on the trunk of *my* Lincoln.

"What do you mean, 'He's in'?" I said. "There's only one guy around here with that kind of power." I pointed with both my thumbs at ol' Johnny Chesthair himself. "And get off of my car, both of ya."

The new guy got right off. Wolf, just too cool, took his time sliding down into his waiting chair like an old movie cowboy and his loyal horsie.

"How'd you get up there, anyway?" I asked.

"Didn't I tell you I could fly?" he said, wise wise wise.

"Well, no, Wolf, you didn't."

"So, just one more thing I got over you, I guess, huh?"

Sigh.

"You." I turned on the prospective new He-Man. Figured I'd better start cracking the whip on *somebody*. "What's your name?"

"Ling-Ling."

"Listen," I barked. "I will dissolve this club *right*

49

now, if you boys don't start getting in line. Now, what's your real name?"

"Ling-Ling."

"Cool," Jerome said. "Like the panda."

"You ain't Chinese," I said.

"I ain't a bear, neither."

"Actually," Jerome chatted away, "a panda isn't a bear at all, it's a—"

"Shaddup," I squawked over Wolfbang's laughter.

However, I realized, he did look like one. A panda. He was about eight feet tall and had an enormous head placed like a beach ball on top of his inflated parade float of a body. He had pale skin and dark circles around his eyes and he was a little ahead of the rest of us in the first-fuzzy-whiskers race, a light coat of cream-colored baby hair that spread evenly over his cheeks and chin, making him look like he was wearing felt on his face. He wore a black hat with fur earflaps, a white sweater, black parka, black jeans, and black boots. Apparently, he was happy to look like a panda.

"Fine, but you want to tell me your real name anyway? Just so, as club brothers, we don't have any secrets from each other?"

"Nope. My real name is confidential, and will remain that way."

"Cool," Jerome said again.

"Weren't you busy quitting or something?" I said to him.

But in fact I agreed. Confidential. Secret. Mysterious. This was good club stuff.

"I don't like it," I said.

Ling-Ling moved to leave. As he brushed past me, I put out my hands to stop him. He was a solid big thing.

"Okay, a trial membership. A special probationary . . . thing."

Ling-Ling shrugged again, a gesture that seemed to mean many different things to him. He took off his coat and hung it on top of Jerome's coat next to Lady Snap-On. Which, by the way, was *my* special coat hook, but I'd address that later.

Ling-Ling then took a walk around the car, checking it out. He just kept nodding his great amazing head. Then he dropped to his hands and knees, looking under the car.

"Frame rot," he said, like I had something trailing out of my nose.

"I'm working on it," I answered defensively.

"Not necessary," Wolf shot. "I'll do it. I'll fix it. I'll make it run. I'll drive it for you. I'm dedicating the rest of my life to this machine."

Since he was Wolfbang, and since he was a wiseguy, you'd figure he was pulling my leg big-time. But his voice and his face said not. We finally found something Wolf liked. The key seemed to be that he just didn't care much for live things.

Ling-Ling then took the liberty of getting into the driver's seat. The *driver's* seat. We all know who the *driver* is and who he isn't, don't we? The Lincoln's old springs cried when Ling squashed them down.

"Jerome," I said as I carefully approached the car to address the problem before it got totally out of control. "What exactly did that little Internet posting say?"

"Um, you know, all the stuff we talked about when we first thought up the club, something like, 'Want to be a real man, hang around with real men, do man stuff? Do you feel like other clubs like the Boy Scouts and the swim team and the Green Berets just don't offer the manly challenges you need? Do you feel like there's a Johnny Chesthair kind of a guy inside you just dying to claw its way out, but you don't even know where to begin? Do laughing girls' voices keep you awake at night? Then come see Steven, and join the He-Man Women Haters Club. No dames, and lots and lots of discipline.'"

I listened to this description of my club. I replayed it in my head. I replayed it again.

"Sounds about right," I said. "But you didn't print an address, just like that, did you?"

"What do you think, I'm a fool? I just posted my Internet address, and fielded responses."

"And?"

"And it was unbelievable. Like, hundreds of responses in the first fifteen minutes. The system crashed." Jerome shook his head, smiling like wasn't this all so cute. "These crazy cyberguys . . ."

"That's just what I was thinking. Jerome, what did you get us into?"

He waved me off. "Stop worrying. When it seemed to me that most of them were a little too . . . excited—you do have to read people carefully out there on the 'Net—I pulled the ad. Ling-Ling was the only normal one, so I gave him the location."

"The only *normal* one . . ." I said, turning back to my sinkin' Lincoln.

I went to the driver's door, and I got right to it.

"Ling-Ling, the first thing is, this is a club of rules. You gotta have rules if you're gonna have anything at all, and we have rules. Second, the rules are made mostly by me, because this is my club, my uncle's garage, and *my* Lincoln. So, one of the biggest rules is, only Steven sits behind the wheel of the Lincoln. You can't sit there."

I automatically took three steps backward, before he even moved anything more than his eyes. Then he turned his whole big face up to me. Then he lifted the great burden of himself out of my poor suffering car. He stared down at me silently, and I did my very best to show him nothing but cold steel eyes in return, even though if he did nothing more than fall on me, I was in deep sneakers.

Then his round chin got all pocked with quivering little wrinkles, and water-balloon tears blobbed from his eyes, up and over his vast cheeks and onto the cement floor.

"All right then," Ling-Ling sobbed. "I'll go."

And go he did, almost. Jerome rushed up beside me, started elbowing me and nudging me after the big baby. Wolf, from the other side of the car, was mouthing, "Go, go."

"What?" I hissed in Jerome's ear. "Am I gonna be spending *all* my club time chasing members down the street and hauling them back inside? Oh right, fun club you got there, Steve-O."

Of course I went anyway. I caught him as he removed his great big jacket from the special hook

54

where it wasn't supposed to be hanging. "It's just a rule, Ling. You don't have to leave."

"No?"

"No. Ain't you ever belonged to anything before?"

He shrugged.

Wolfbang tried to help, in his way. "Ya, Ling. Like, in my residential facility where I'm a resident, they got millions of rules, rules on everything, posted on the walls, in this little handbook—so many rules, you could choke. *No biting the staff . . . Clothes must be worn in the hallways at all times. . . . No hanging yourself in the stairwell . . .* It's like, no freedom. This is nothing."

I stared at Wolf without saying anything. Back to Ling. "You know, like *anything* where they had rules or dos and don'ts or whatever? Ever been in anything like that at all?"

"Um, like with a lot of other people, you mean."

"Ya, like that, only it doesn't even have to be a lot."

"No? How many then, minimum, would you mean?"

I tipped a glance toward Jerome, feeling that the strangeness of the conversation would fall into his club jurisdiction.

"Two, Ling," Jerome said. "I think two, anyway, would be the minimum of what we could call a group."

He nodded his head. "Well then, no, I've never actually belonged to one."

I hot-stepped right over and grrred into Jerome's ear. "You're responsible for this. We couldn't even get rid of him now if we wanted to, because he'd probably kill himself."

Jerome smiled at Ling, then whispered, "Or us."

"That's it," I said. "You are officially club vice president in charge of Ling-Ling. Congratulations."

"Fine," he said. "I like him."

I almost clipped him. But I supposed if I could work on old Ling, he could turn out to be mighty useful. Or, at least, mighty. Ling was some serious bulk to add to our troops.

"So okay then, Ling? Don't sweat it. You can sit in the backseat of the car. It's not like the cars they build today; this is a huge, comfortable backseat. Go ahead and try it out."

Silently, he agreed. He pulled a rolled log of superhero comic books out of the inside pocket of his parka, then went to hang the jacket back on the nail.

"Oh, and by the way," I said, perhaps not at the

best time, "that hook is also off limits. That is my hook, and you have to find another place for your—"

He started crying again.

This time it didn't make me feel bad or nervous. Now it was making me angry.

"Oh, please, could you do that in the corner or something?" I actually started pushing him from behind, like a car stuck in the snow. "There ya go, back there somewhere. Ya, in the car, take your magazines . . . there you go."

When Ling was safe and soggy in the back of the car—I dumped Wolf in there to keep him company and slammed the door behind them—I turned on Jerome.

"See? Computers. They stink. Only ginks and bizarros use computers and I'm passing a no-computers rule right now. I'll come to your house and smash that computer with my head, if you do that again."

"Like you could do better. At least my way we get members who can read."

"Ya, well, that's not important in this club," I said. And meant it.

7
Right All Along

"Get over here," my uncle said to me, and pulled me off to a neutral corner. "Just exactly what kind of a club you got going here, anyway?" I had my back to the guys and as he spoke Lars kept shooting looks at them over my shoulder, as if he feared they were going to make a move on him if he didn't watch it.

I shrugged. It was all a little hard to define. "It's a guy thing," I said.

"I can see that," he said harshly. "It's what kinda guys, and what kinda things, I'm curious about. 'Cause when I seen that new one come strollin' in the other day—*Ling-Ling*, for cryin' out loud?—I says to myself, I says, whoa now . . . and in addition to that Jerome kid who I had my doubts about from the get-go, when the Girl Scouts kicked the livin'—"

"Uncle Lars, do you think you could put this in the form of a question?"

"Is this a Sally Sweetboys' club you got here, or what?"

I should have seen, from the funny way he was pronouncing his words at me, to the way all the color had drained from his already light-gray face, to the violent way he was looking at Jerome. . . . I should have seen where he was headed. But I didn't. I didn't because . . . because it was just so far from the planet reality. Me? ME? *Me?* I was floored.

"Course not, stupid. It's a Johnny Chesthair kind of a club."

He stopped, stared at the guys some more. Torqued his head like dogs do when you give them commands they don't understand.

"All right then," he said cautiously. "If you say so, Steven. It's just they look . . . and I'd still like to see youse get yourselves into a fight or somethin', somethin' wholesome."

"We're working on it," I said.

In fact, we were working on it not five minutes later. But I don't think it was the kind of fight he had in mind.

The doorbell in the garage clanged like a thousand electrified cowbells, making everybody jump and putting every one of us in a nasty mood. Lars said the bell had to be that loud to be heard over the power tools. Nobody ever used it anyway. Almost nobody.

"It's open, ya fool," Lars screamed, louder than the bell.

The door creaked open, and as I looked up, it was as if my Haunts had split wide open and spilled into my regular, formerly well-ordered daytime life.

But this was not a Haunt. It only played like one.

Monica, in her Girl Scout outfit—did she sleep in the thing, or what?—came strolling in, wearing a smile as wide as the grille on an old Cadillac. Her hair, which was usually so wild and ferocious that it couldn't fit inside one of those Cat-in-the-Hat hats, was pulled into two hard braids framing and taming her face. Like when the devil fools everybody by hiding his tail inside a nice suit. She was carrying a shopping bag with her two hands joined together in front of her, with those fuzzy white alpaca mittens that make her look harmless.

See, this is *exactly* what I've been talking about. No rules. *No rules* whatsoever. Monica is here, in my space, in my place, the very spot on this earth that is dedicated to the defense of decent guys like me against the dark-hearted, unpredictable, sweet-smelling, evil empire of the likes of Monica and her ilk. *She was not supposed to come here. And she knew that. She knew it. She knew it. That's why she came.*

"Code red, guys, code red!" I yelped as I tore for the front of the shop.

Wolf was lying on a dolly, rolled completely underneath the car. Jerome was passing him tools and flashlights and Fig Newtons. Ling was inside the car reading *X-Men.* None raced to my side.

Lars was slumped over a Subaru and didn't look up.

"Watch out!" I hollered at Lars as I ran to help him with the Red Menace.

He leaped, froze himself into tae kwon do readiness. Then he looked down at Monica. Went back to work without addressing her.

"I think you can handle this crisis on your own, Steven," he said.

Sweating, I almost blurted the truth, which was: I think I can't.

"What are you doing here?" I said to her.

"I'm selling cookies," she said sweetly.

Grrrrr.

"Ya, well, we don't need your kind of cookies around here," I said.

By then, my trusty clubmates had reached the scene.

"Ya," Jerome said. "We don't need your kind of cookies."

Monica refused to stop smiling.

"I like cookies," Wolf said.

I turned on him, to shoot him a withering stare that would bring him back in line. He never even noticed.

"Hey, Steven," Wolf said, still looking at Monica. "What do we got in petty cash? Can we swing a box of cookies?"

"No," I snapped.

Ling returned to the car when I ruled out the cookies.

"Why do you come all the way over here to sell those stupid cookies anyhow?" I asked. "I heard you . . . people were selling your rotten cookies by mail and over computer and stuff. And even if you weren't, nobody ever comes *here* to sell nothing."

"Hey," Lars snapped.

Somehow, Monica managed to widen that smile. "I heard there was a new club or something on the premises, so while we have never been able to sell *anything* at this location before . . ."

"Heh-heh-heh-heh," chuckled Lars proudly.

". . . I thought there might be some hungry young men here who might like a snack."

62

"I might like a snack," Wolf chimed in.

"A smack, did you say?" I answered. Then I turned to my second-in-command. "Jerome, wheel this guy out of here."

Jerome circled around behind Wolf and started pulling on the handles of the wheelchair. Nothing. Wolfbang held on to the wheels, and Jerome was no match. Wolf barely noticed, smiling away at Monica, as Jerome sweated and grunted and climbed all over the chair trying to carry out his duty, like he was trying to pull Excalibur out of a rock.

"Wow, this is impressive," she said to me. The little troublemaker. "You really are the general around here."

Wolf cut in, which was fine, since all I could do at that point was blush so hard I reflected pink off the ceiling.

"Ooooohh, I don't know about this, General. Are the rules that we gotta hate *all* women, or can we make exceptions? Can we get a ruling on this, 'cause I just don't think I'm gonna be able to hate this one. Nope, just don't think I can manage it. I'll just have to pay the fine or whatever."

"You're sweet," Monica said to the rat in our midst.

At that instant, something started bubbling up in my stomach, and I had never felt anything like it before. Like I'd eaten live bees. I looked at Wolfbang, and the bees tore the lining out of my belly.

"Can I have a free box of cookies, if I'm sweet?" Wolf asked.

Buzzzbuzzzbuzzzbuzzz. I didn't even know why this should bother me. What did I care if he talked to her?

She shook her head no.

The buzzing quieted.

He shrugged. Then, as Jerome was about to give up, his asthma inhaler hanging out of his mouth like a cigar, Wolf let go of the wheels, and the two of them shot in reverse toward the Lincoln.

"I will see you to the door," I said sternly, in my General voice.

I pushed the door open to let her out, and boosted myself slightly up on my toes to narrow the difference in height as she brushed by.

"Perhaps your club and my club can get together sometime," she said, stopping right there, inches away, with the two of us squashed in the doorway. Touching, practically. "I think that might be fun, don't you?"

Wicked, wicked, foul evil thing. She'll spring her tail as soon as the door shuts behind her.

"Hnnn," I said, which wasn't exactly clever but did end the conversation.

Then, just before stepping out into the street, Monica slipped one fuzzy mitt down into the bag, shoved a box into my hands, and dashed off.

The door slammed behind her. I looked at the box.

Tagalongs.

Wicked, wicked, foul evil thing. No rules for them. They'll do anything. Can't take your eyes off them for a second.

I cracked the door open just enough to check her out as she went back to her own self and sprouted her tail. Instead, I saw her gang, three other savage, bloodthirsty girls who had been lying out there in their snipers' nest, and now were laughing and squealing, and pulling on Monica's arms, demanding, "More. What happened then? What did he do? What did he say?"

So, I was right all along. It was a conspiracy.

8

Johnny Junior

"Give it some more gas, Dad."

He raced the engine. The fan nearly cut off my brand-new Adam's apple.

"I didn't say to race it," I hollered over the noise.

After I had adjusted the idle on the carburetor for the hundredth time, and got the engine running high enough so that it could sustain life on its own without me under the hood, I closed it and circled around to the window. The old man handed me a dollar. Sport.

"You know, Dad, you might want to invest in a new set of spark plugs, distributor cap, oil change, instead of just having me keep turning the engine up higher."

"C'mon," he said. "Why would I do all that when I got you? You love doing this stuff." He punched me in the chest, knocking me four feet away. I walked back to where I was.

"Don't be hitting him all the time, Buster," my mom said from her seat next to him. "I think his chest is sinking in from it." She wasn't getting tough with him—no, no, *nobody* does that. Buster is really his name. At least that's what he's always called himself.

"*Pffft,*" he said, thumping me in the very same, hollow-sounding midpoint of my chest, sending me back again. I walked the long walk back to him, like one of those inflatable Bozo dummies that keep bouncing up for more beatings. "Boys love this stuff. I could hit him all day, and he'd just laugh." He hadn't noticed that I never actually did laugh at it.

The car started wheezing, fading again. I shook my head as Buster responded by abusing the gas pedal some more.

Vrrrroooom! said the desperate car.

"I love that sound," said the driver. "Don't you love that sound, Steven?"

"It sounds like you're breaking it," my mother accurately observed.

He thumb-jerked at her. "Don't listen to the driver's side airbag over there. She's just a girl. She don't understand what we understand."

As he began backing down the driveway, he

67

called me with a wagging finger. Like I was on a leash, I followed the car down to the street as he kept right on backing. There he stopped.

"I hear about that club you got goin', down there at the shop."

"Ya," I said, making a mental note to punch my uncle Lars in the stomach.

"I hear your club's maybe got some freaks in it. Like, a freak club. Maybe a Sally Sweetboy club."

I updated my mental note, to punch Lars elsewhere.

"No way, Dad. You know me. It's a Johnny Chesthair kind of a club."

He cuffed me. The cuff with a smile.

"That's good. I knew that's what it'd be. You wouldn't dare turn sweetboy on me, I know that. But you know, Swimmer, there's only one Johnny Chesthair around here, right?"

"Right, Dad."

"That is such a disgusting-sounding name," Mom said.

He didn't hear her, even though he did. "And that makes you . . ."

"Johnny junior," I said, like a good son.

Buster laughed, punched me in the chest, rolled up his window, and shot away.

I closed one eye, aimed with my finger, and *I* shot away. Blew out both rear tires. The car flipped over, slammed into the pumps at Hector's BP gas station. Burst into monster flames. Mom crawled from the wreck unharmed. She walked home alone and made me a snack.

"Have you been here since I left you on Sunday?" I asked Ling-Ling, who sure looked like he had been. He was sitting slumped in the back of the Lincoln, head about three inches above his knees, which held a stack of comics. He looked up.

"Of course I haven't," he said, then went back to reading.

We were the first two there, as would become standard. We met at the club on Saturdays in the morning, and on Tuesday, Thursday, and Friday afternoons. I always beat Jerome and Wolfbang to the meetings. I rarely beat Ling.

"Think I could have a look at some of those?" I asked.

He quickly thumbed the deck, as if he were taking inventory, figured he was holding two dozen magazines, and decided he could spare two. One *Batman*, one *Wolverine*.

"You're really into these, huh, Ling?"

He looked up at me, squinting, a puzzled look. "Well, why wouldn't I be? Comic books—the real ones, anyway—they're only what *everything* is all about. I mean, like *Wolverine*, sheesh." He snorted a little chuckle through his fleshy panda nose, as if we were talking about what everybody should know. Like Abe Lincoln and honesty, or Michael Jordan and basketball. "*Wolverine* is the whole story, the *whole* story of man, right there."

I stared down at it, held it feathery in my hand, weighing it. It wasn't even fifty pages, for crying out loud.

"You're nuts," Lars said into Ling-Ling's open window.

"Beat it, you," I snapped. "This is a private club and you are not welcome, ya rat."

He stepped back from the car. "What's got into you, neph?"

"What did you tell my old man?"

"Nothin'."

"Rat. Lying rat."

Ling-Ling dropped his head and went back to reading while we argued across him.

"Lars, did you tell my father I had some kind of freak club down here or didn't you?"

Lars blushed. "Oh, that. Listen, kid, all I said was—"

"Rat. What did you go and tell him that for?"

Ling looked up at me, totally serious, totally calm. "Well, you do, right?"

"Arrrrgh," I said. The club was already making me say that so much, I was thinking of making "Arrrrgh" our motto.

"I never said you were freaks," he answered. "All I said was I was concerned. Curious. You know your old man, he overreacts, that's all. So I had to promise him I'd look out for you, and provide a little right-thinking guidance, and he was cool with that. You're lucky. He might have broke up your club if I didn't promise to show you boys the Way."

"Super," I said sarcastically.

"And I think I should start with this." He whipped the *X-Men* comic book right out of Ling-Ling's hand. Without a stutter, Ling just went right on, turning to page one of the next mag on the pile. "This," Lars said, "is not what it's all about. Jeez, you guys really are such kids, ain't ya? This stuff, it ain't life, it's baby food. Wait here, I'll show you what it's *really* all about."

Lars bolted toward the front of the shop, passed Wolfbang and Jerome on their way in, and disappeared into his office. Then he ran back out waving some magazines of his own, passed the two slowpokes again, and tossed me and Ling each a magazine. Ling-Ling held his up. It was *Soldier of Fortune*. Mine was *American Survival Guide,* subtitled *The Magazine of Self-Reliance.*

Hmmmm.

"*Wolverine*'s tougher," Ling-Ling said, and tossed me his magazine.

"You're dreamin', kid," Lars shot back. "You don't know nothin'."

"That's not very helpful," I said to Lars. "For a guy who's supposed to be giving us guidance."

"Okay, then. Kid—what's your name?"

Ling told him.

"Still stickin' with that story, huh?"

"That's the name."

"Right then, that's cool. My code name with the Survivors is Hollow Tip. So here goes, Hollow Tip versus Ling-Ling, your magazine against mine."

There were lots of times I did not follow what was going on in my uncle's head. There were other times when I did and thought it was cool. There were still other times when I thought he was out of his skull. But all the time, he was so sure and so excited about whatever it was that was going on up there that you just had to cut him a little slack for enthusiasm points.

However, he could still embarrass a guy for being related to him.

"My magazine could mop the joint with yours," Lars said to Ling.

Wolfbang had wheeled up tight to the action, bumping into the back of Lars's legs. "Get him, Ling!" he cheered, without knowing, or caring, what was going on. "Get him, Ling, get him, Ling."

"What's going on?" Jerome said, sliding into the front seat. Jerome, of course, needed to know. I waved him to shut up.

Ling looked to me. I shrugged.

"Get him, Ling," I said.

"Wolverine is a *man*, Lars, okay? He does all his own fighting. And he fights for what's right."

"Fighting?" my middle-aged uncle wheezed. "You call that fighting? Kid, you're talking about car*toons* there. Your Wolverine fights cartoons. Even *I* could fight a cartoon and win. Even *you* could fight a cartoon and win. Jeesh."

Lars was never any good at jokes, so the thing here was, he was serious.

"These boys here, well, just look at them. *Soldier of Fortune,* boys, soak it up, because it's the future, it's the now. It's life as we're gonna know it in this country. The men in that magazine"—here Lars broke off into a little spooky uncontrollable laugh for himself, *h-h-h-heh-hah*—"those are *the* men of this country. And they ain't no cartoon men, lemme tell ya that right now."

Ling stopped looking at Lars, turning instead to me for translation. I hadn't a clue. I turned to Jerome, hoping he might be able to wrap his big juicy brain around my uncle's logic.

"I don't know," said Jerome, taking up my copy of *American Survival Guide*. "They sure do look like cartoons to me."

I leaned in closer to look over Jerome's shoulder as he browsed. He was right. The pictures running with articles like "Getting the Most Out of Body Armor" and "Primitive Living Challenge" sure did look awfully G.I. Joe. Big puffed-up guys. Big puffed-up gals. Staring down the camera like they were going to bite it. Muscled outdoorspeople, pack animals, electronics for the field, pads and armor and camouflage and cool ranger hats and guns. Guns. Guns, that is. Did I forget to say guns? The guns were just too big and too shiny and too accessorized to be for real. The centerfold—yup, they had a centerfold—was a picture of some kind of weapon that had a handle on it, so I supposed

74

somebody was supposed to hold the thing in one hand, but it seemed to me that anyone with a hand big enough and strong enough to hold that thing didn't need any weapon of any kind. I slapped the magazine closed and held it down, like the contents could blast their way out if somebody didn't keep them in there.

"This is actually kind of scary, Lars," Jerome said.

"This is actually kind of *awesome*," Wolfbang said, lapping up *Soldier of Fortune* like it was a girlie mag. "You don't actually know people like this, do you?"

Lars folded his arms across his caved-in little chest area. "*Know* people like that? Boy, I happen to *be* people like that."

"This is the *best* club," Wolf said, pumping his fist. "Except we still need to get that redhead cookie girl back."

The bees. The angry bees, I guess, were set up for good in my belly, because every time Wolfbang mentioned Monica . . . it made the buzzing unbearable.

"Shaddup, you," I warned.

"Oooo," Wolf taunted. "Got a little problem there, Tagalong?"

I lunged for him. "Don't call me that. Don't you call me that. And don't you ever . . ."

Wolf and I were sitting, together, in his wheelchair, clawing and choking and slapping at each other and not really accomplishing anything. My uncle grabbed me by the back of the shirt. Then he wagged a finger at me. "Not over a *dame*," he scolded.

Just like Darla and Alfalfa and Spanky. I panicked.

"No way, sludge monkey. Not this boy."

Wolf snickered.

"Can we get back to important club business?" Ling cut in. "Our man Lars here . . ."

I couldn't let it get away from me like this. "What are you talking about? He's not in the club, ya dope. He's a"—long pause for total disgust effect—"grown-up geezer. Get out of here, will ya, Lars."

"I might be a geezer, but I know what's what in a he-man's world. And you boys could sure learn a lesson. You want a lesson?"

"No," I snapped, even though he wasn't addressing me.

"Sure," Wolf piped.

I looked to Jerome, who stared up at Lars with big baby-seal, don't-club-me eyes.

"Cartoon boy, what do ya say?" Lars asked Ling-Ling. Ling looked like he might cry, which would have surprised no one.

"Show me," Ling bellowed in a mighty sure voice, which surprised everyone.

"This is my club," I raved as I followed the rest of them out to Lars's car. "I'm the boss, remember? You don't just run off with another guy without my say-so. We need order! We need rules here!"

Wolfbang's wheels skidded on the oily garage floor as he braked to a stop. He spun to face me. He sighed loudly.

"So, can we go, Dad?"

I was caught by surprise. Stumped. I wanted to scream some more. I wasn't finished screaming yet. I thought.

"Bus is leaving, children," Lars called.

"It's going to be so crowded in his car," I muttered. "His stupid car is so . . . not like *my* car. My car is big, and roomy and strong and . . ."

"His car *runs*," Jerome pointed out.

"Shaddup over there. Mine's going to run. Just wait. When I—"

"Steven," Ling called, very impatiently. "Are you going to come or not?" It seemed awfully important all of a sudden to Ling.

"Not," I said.

Without hesitation Lars, Wolf, and Ling were out the door. Jerome stood there waiting.

"Couldn't hurt, you know, Steven," he said. "It might even be interesting, whatever it is he wants to show us. Are you afraid of something you're not telling us? I mean, he is your uncle, right? Your father's brother? Is there a fair chance he's going to drive us all off a cliff or sell us to a circus or something? If he is, you should tell us, I think. And if he's not . . ." Jerome shrugged. "We joined up for adventure, right?" A squiggly scared smile cracked across his face.

"No, Lars is okay. It's just . . . it's my club. Is it or isn't it my club?"

Just then Lars cranked his car, a sonic boom of straight, unmuffled pipes. Jerome jumped.

"It's your club, Steven. Everybody knows who Johnny Chesthair is around here."

The smoothie.

"But still, we kind of want to *do* stuff, you know?"

"I guess," I said. Without even agreeing to, I started following Jerome out the door.

I felt it happening to me as I went out. That I was going from being the head of the dog to being the tail. I was even walking with a slight side-to-side waggle. I had to hold on to something here.

"But *I* get to ride in the front seat," I insisted.

"You're the boss," Jerome said.

9
Captains America

Field trip. Lars couldn't bear the lame condition of my club.

"Buckle up, young Americans. My club is going to show you-all the way."

I thought he meant it as a figure of speech, like "*buck* up." You never can tell with Lars. But no, he meant it literally. He slammed his foot down on the accelerator and whooped as he took the hard corners of the city at forty miles per hour. He lit a cigarette, beeped his horn at nothing. He nearly clipped a pedestrian, but then didn't bother beeping. He screamed. He laughed at himself. He created an odor. Laughed at himself again. When all the passengers were nearly asphyxiated, I tapped him on the shoulder and he finally opened the window. Did I mention that the driver's window was the only one that worked? Somebody in a worse car than Lars's made a left turn across

80

his path. He beeped and beeped and gestured and screamed until long after the person was probably parked and eating dinner at home. Every bolt in the car shook as Lars demanded much more of the vehicle than was probably fair.

We screeched to a stop.

Jerome vomited out into the street.

Lars stepped past Jerome and his mess, stared at it. "What are those in there, Alpha-Bits? Well, no wonder you're sick, that stuff's no good for ya."

"What are we doing?" I asked as my uncle pulled the wheelchair out of the trunk. We were parked in front of a dilapidated used-auto-parts yard with a twelve-foot fence surrounding a small lot and a cinderblock bunker of a building. Even by junkyard standards, the place was a pit.

"We're going into my club," he said. "Don't let appearances fool ya. These are the kind of people who like to keep a low-down profile, but the true fact is that these guys in here are the greatest collection of Americans in . . . in America, anyway. There's, like, the modern Paul Revere inside here . . . the contemporary Patrick Henry . . . John Wayne . . . the whole shebang of American patriotic history." Lars brought the wheelchair around to the door, where Wolf climbed in. "You," he said, pointing then to

Ling-Ling. "Now, my man, is when you are going to meet some superheroes. Every one of them is a Captain America."

"I think I'm going to sit in the car," Jerome said.

I went over and pulled him out by the wrist. "You're the one who got me into the club business," I said.

Wolfbang was struggling, his skinny wheels spinning over the rough terrain of the yard. But he seemed to enjoy the rough going, like one of those four-wheel-drive nuts in mud. Ling had him beat, though, brushing by him and practically running up Lars's back to get into that building and the Captains America Club.

It took us a little longer, with me pulling Jerome like a sled over dry pavement, but finally we joined everyone inside. The members of my club stood thunderstruck, silent, watching the members of Lars's club hug and growl and slap each other hard.

They looked like they'd stepped straight out of the pages of Lars's magazines.

We met Kevin, in his red-and-black–checked wool jacket, unbuttoned down to his naked belly. Jimma, who was wearing the T-shirt that Kevin was not wearing, topped off with a . . . thing, like a vest with straps and pads all over it. Boo, who was as large and bearlike as Ling-Ling, only with a face so scarred up it looked like a car had been dropped on it. Since Boo was wearing filthy coveralls and was apparently the garage owner, this may have been possible.

And we met Officer Timmy, who wore a crisp dark-blue outfit, shiny black shoes, and enough medals and ribbons across his chest for a king or a fancy hotel doorman.

"Are you a police officer or a military officer, Officer Timmy?" Wolf asked.

OT looked down on Wolfbang in his chair, as if he hadn't seen him until that moment, and made a face. You know the face. He was disgusted either with Wolf's question or his voice or—from the way he was looking him over—his disability.

"I am an officer of my god," he sneered, "and of my country."

"Ooooohhh-kaaayyy," Wolf said, smirking.

Jerome was quick in my ear. "That's it. Really, this time, I quit. Don't bother to see me to the door—"

"Shhhh," I said. "He might hear you."

"Heroes," Lars sang. "Kids, I hope you realize how lucky you are. You want to be men? You want

83

to run a club called He-Man? Here's your proto-type."

I looked around at our prototype. I looked at Lars to see if he was kidding. Not. I looked at my guys. Wolf had his hand over his mouth but wasn't trying too hard to hide his laughter. Ling was mes-merized, entranced, looking at the place, the faces, the scars, the uniforms of one kind and another. Yes, Ling was taking this very seriously. I looked at Jerome. Jerome looked at me. Jerome bolted.

"Hey, come back, Jerome," I called. But by the time I got to the flung-open door, he was halfway home, bounding like a gazelle over moving cars and pedestrians and everything.

" 'Bye, Mary," Kevin called. "Come see us again soon, ya stud."

Jimma, with the padded vest, stepped up to me. "I could track him. You want me to track him for you? I usually charge, but since you're with ol' Lars . . ."

I stepped back, shook my head no. "That's all right," I said. "I think we'll let him go this time."

"You let me know, you change your mind," Jimma said.

On the desk near the door, a small black-and-white TV buzzed, the screen doing one long nonstop horizontal somersault. It was a talk show playing, with a very neat-looking blond lady named Wendy Wightman talking to a married couple who lived in an abandoned oil tank.

Lars went around then like a matchmaker. "This is the magazine kid," he said, literally shoving Ling-Ling toward Boo. Boo smiled, looking down at the literature in Ling's hand. "I started out with Marvel comics myself. It's a good start. *However* . . ." and the two of them pulled over to a corner, where Boo broke out a crate of his own preferred reading.

"Watch out for him, Kevin," Lars said as Wolfbang paired off with him. "He's a handful. Wicked mouth on him, bad attitude."

Kevin didn't mind, since Kevin was *their* Wolfbang. "Ya? Well his mouth may be wicked, but his legs ain't showin' me much."

Wolf laughed so hard that one of his legs started doing a wild, jumpy dance right there, out of control. Kevin was pleased, slapping his belly with one hand, pointing at the leg with the other. "Want me to shoot it for ya? If it's giving ya trouble, we should shoot the sucker."

"Sure," Wolf said. But I don't think he meant it.

"You know, it don't bother me none, you being

in that chair. Sixty percent of all my friends are in wheelchairs too. That's a fact."

"Great," Wolf said. "Then you're a pro at this. Run, get a sponge and give me my sponge bath."

"I love this kid," Kevin wheezed.

It was like I was sitting outside the principal's office, only worse. There were limits to what a principal was allowed to do to a kid. I pretended not to notice as I saw Lars and somebody coming my way. Instead I pretended fascination at the decor of the room. The American flag taking up one wall. The Snap-On Tools Girl with a great big pneumatic gun pointed right at me. A framed, glass-covered picture of Ronald Reagan, who by that time was I think like seven or eight presidents ago.

"Here's your man," I heard Lars saying to Officer Timmy.

He saluted me. I saluted back. But mostly I stared. Spanning the width of him from shoulder to shoulder were his full-size silver chrome badges. *Concealed Weapons Permit. United Nations Security. Federal Firearms License. Professional Firefighter. Bail Enforcement Agent. Special Agent. Military Intelligence. CIA. Sergeant, Los Angeles Police, Badge #714 (Dragnet,* the TV show).

"Go ahead," Timmy said, correctly estimating my reading speed, "ask me a question."

"You actually held all those . . . jobs?"

"Held 'em," he said.

It seemed, at that point, like we'd pretty much exhausted all we had to talk about. Timmy wasn't a chatter. Man-of-action type, naturally. And I had reached my conclusion anyhow.

Total, over-the-top, why-is-this-man-out-loose nutbag.

But those badges *were* awfully nice.

"I can see it in you," Timmy said, yanking me out of the trance caused by my staring into the reflection of my own eye in the chrome. "You are a leader without portfolio. Am I right?"

"You might be," I said. "What's a portfolio?"

"What I'm saying is, *you* know that you are a leader among men, but sometimes it seems others are slow to recognize that fact. Am I right?"

My mouth fell open. I had heard about this thing where totally insane people have pretty strong insight into the rest of us, but I never thought it could be this true. Or this specific.

"Ya," I said. "How . . . ?"

"I wasn't *born* at the top," Timmy said. "I had my struggles. There was a time when people had trouble taking orders from me. There was a time when people failed to recognize in me the qualities of a leader. There was a time when I couldn't get a cab . . . or a driver's license . . . or a date to a stinking rotten semiformal . . ."

"Officer?" I interrupted gently. "I'm connected in this story here someplace, is that right?"

"Huh?" he said, as if I'd just made that up. "Oh. Ya, you are. Your uncle here tells me you started this here club, which is good. Tells me you named it He-Man Women Haters, which is very good, shows you know what's what at a very young age. Country needs more guys like you. Country needs more men, period." He looked down at his own chest, scanning it. Then he selected a badge, removed it, and pinned it on me.

"I want you to know," OT said, his voice breaking, "that this badge is something special. This was the one—and I got mine way back when *Dragnet* was the greatest *American* television show ever, and not that stupid movie that made fun of everything that's good about America—this was the badge that started to make all the difference for me. And I'm giving it to you because I have so much respect for this man over here." He pointed to Lars. "Who I hope you realize is one of the greatest living American patriots alive in America today. I'd kill for this man."

I believed he would.

I didn't take my eyes off his steely, unpleasant face the whole time, since I had no idea what was going on here. But when he stepped back and admired my chest—and saluted me with a little more respect this time—I was moved to look down.

I was the LAPD sergeant.

I looked around the room to see if everyone had fallen to their knees. It suddenly occurred to me that everyone in *their* club had a mustache.

Wolf was laughing again at whatever Kevin was saying. "Get out!" Wolf said. "Liar. *Nothing*'s that big."

Ling looked like he was a monk in Tibet, actually kneeling at the feet of this Boo character, poring over his texts and absorbing his wisdom.

"I was once like you," Officer Timmy said to me. "And I wouldn't ever want to be *that* again."

Thanks for your support there, officer.

"Now I'm Officer Timmy. And everybody knows it." He tapped me on the badge with his thick yellow index fingernail. "Mark my words. You'll see."

Ya, well, I hope I never see what *you* see, is what I was thinking as I shook his hand. But like a laser beam, that badge kept on pulling my eye back down. My, it was an impressive thing.

"So, like a club, right? What do you all do?" Wolf asked all of them at once. "I mean, you sell candy and raffle tickets and have dances and Fourth of July picnics and stuff?"

"What are you talking about? What are you asking?" said Jimma as he walked back in from wrecking cars out in the yard.

"I'm asking what do you *do* here. You, like, have parties, or what?"

"*This* is a party," Jimma said, in a very unpartylike tone of voice.

Wolfbang was never one to be intimidated, even when he should have been. "Ya, well, while this is really a swinging time and all, is this it? And what about girls?"

Jeez, Wolfbang, would you get off the girls already?

It was like Wolf had spat at the guy.

"*Well, what about 'em, then? We like 'em! Like 'em a lot. Like 'em plenty! Who told you to ask us that?*"

"We just don't like 'em *here*," Kevin added.

This seemed like not a bad time to go.

"Boy," Wolf said when we were all back in the car. "Good thing *we*'re not nuts like them, huh?" But he was laughing hysterically when he said it.

10
The High Dive

While Jerome clearly wanted no part of the Captains America—and who could blame him, really—he still seemed to want all kinds of parts of me.

Winter was finally melting away, which meant it was time for me to get back in the water. I was counting on the coach to have forgotten about my chest hairs, but how likely was that? I had a lot on my mind.

"No club today, Jerome," I said as the last bell rang and I headed for the pool.

Jerome followed right behind me, carrying a bag that looked suspiciously like mine. "I know that, silly."

I looked him over. "Where are you going?"

"Same place you're going."

"Come on, Jerome," I said. "You don't want to be swim team manager anymore."

"You're right, I don't."

"So then what . . . ?"

It takes me a while sometimes, but I do catch on.

"No, Jerome, no, no."

"Yes, Steven, yes, yes. Listen, you didn't come up with a sport for me, so I came up with one for myself. And it makes perfect sense. I can do this. It'll be cool."

"I was thinking, maybe soccer, Jerome. Y'know, it's kind of for weenies, but it's a start, you know. . . ."

He shook his head determinedly. "I'm going splashing with *you*."

Jeez, I thought, if my old man ever gets a load of this . . .

But I got used to the idea pretty quickly. Jerome was getting better and better to have around. He certainly paid more attention to me when I spoke and had more respect for what I said than . . . anyone else in my whole entire life. So hanging out more, being on the team together, might turn out to be cool enough.

We sat on benches in the locker room, listening to the coach's Welcome to Spring Swimming speech. I kept my shirt on to delay as long as possible before I unleashed the Jungle. Jerome was stripped down to nothing but his suit, and was so excited about his

93

new adventure that he kept popping up, slapping himself on the arms, sitting again, slapping his skinny thighs. He looked like a chihuahua.

"As you may have noticed," coach said, "the school has not for the last few years had a girls' swim team—"

"Ya!" Jerome spouted.

"That's enough of that, you," coach said. "Well, that's because there was simply no demand from the students. The administration, the school board, the courts, have all made it clear that, if there is any interest in girls' athletics, the school is required to provide equal opportunity . . ."

Oh no. No, no.

". . . and this term, it turns out that there is some interest, but not quite enough to warrant a separate girls' team. Therefore . . ."

We walked out of the boys' locker room, through the entrance to the pool, following the coach like a duck family. And when we got out there and found Monica suited up and ready to rumble, I was so deflated I would have sunk to the bottom if they threw me in the water.

"Hi, Steven," she chirped. "I didn't know you were on the swim team."

There are ninety kids in the school. Everybody

knows what's in everybody's *lunch* every day.

"Ya," I said. "Well, I still haven't decided whether I'm going to stay."

"Oh, please do," she said. "I bet you're the best on the team."

Jerome jacked in so tight behind me, I could count his ribs from their impression on my back. "Remember Darla, Steven. Remember no-good Darla," he whispered.

"You," she snapped at him. "That is *so* rude, what you're doing back there. Why don't you just grow up."

I turned all the way around to get a look at Jerome's little bat face. I gave him a so-what-are-you-going-to-do-about-it look.

"Oh ya?" he hissed at Monica. "Well, we don't need you anyway. So stop wasting Steven's time, you wicked redheaded . . . stork."

Monica gasped. I myself was a little thrown.

"Hey, Jerome," I said. "You don't have to be so—"

"We have a whole club dedicated to practically nothing else but hating you, so what do you think of that?"

"Jerome, I think that's enough—" I said nervously.

"No," Monica said, smiling the old scary smile. "Please, do finish."

"I will," Jerome rambled on. "It's called the He-Man Women Haters Club, and old Johnny Chesthair here is the . . ."

I don't even recall what he said after that. The last impression I have is of Monica with both hands covering her mouth as she convulsed with laughter and I—being the strong and quick-thinking leader of men—threw myself into the pool. I hung under there, as close to the bottom as possible, for as long as I could, hoping to either pass out or breach through the surface of the water to find it was all a sick dream and had gone away.

I breached, all right. Into a world where Monica and her friend Tory—the other new recruit who was not at all a guy—and all of my old teammates were filling the building with the hysterical sound of a dozen lunatic dolphins.

Coach had noticed that I'd jumped into the water with my shirt on. He came to the side of the pool.

"Lift up that shirt," he grouched. "I have to check something."

I slithered out of the water and right past him on my way back to the locker room.

"You don't have to see," I said. "Just ask *them*."

11

What Do You Want, a Badge or a Chest to Pin It On?

It was the thing that gave me strength now, through trying times, and I kept it close to my heart.

"Steven," Mom asked cautiously, "what exactly is that?"

"It's a badge," I said, craning my neck down to breathe on it, then buffing it with my shirtsleeve.

"Are you a policeman?" She handed me a plate of sunny-side ups, their googly yellow eyes wide with respect for me.

"Not quite. It's a club thing. A guy thing. You wouldn't understand."

She took the seat next to me at the kitchen table. "I'd like to. Try me. Tell me about this club your father keeps raving on about."

"He does? He raves? About me, and my club? What does he say—not that it matters to me—but, what does he say, what does he say?"

"It doesn't matter, Steven. You know your father . . . he's crazy, that's just his way. Pay him no—"

"Ma?"

"Fine. He says it's about time you joined the man's world."

I sat for a few seconds trying to form a response. But first I had to figure out whether it was a compliment or a rip.

"So . . . he's glad, right, Ma?"

"Oh yes, very supportive."

"Great!" I yelped. Then, much cooler, "Not that it really matters."

"Not that it does, no. But now I'm curious, son. In your own words, in one sentence, what is this organization about?"

Now, there was always something about my mother, a sort of tiredness about her, I guess. And it was contagious. She could look into you with those weary cow eyes, and you wanted to just go back to bed, or maybe cry if you looked too close. Don't know where she got it from, if it was a medical condition or if it was just her *way*, like she herself always says a person has a *way* about them. And I don't think I want to know, either, because most of the time I can squiggle around it so that it

98

doesn't affect me, doesn't pull me too far down into it with her. But like here, when she asks me something that for whatever screwy reason seems to be important to her, she has this way about her, of biting her lip and widening her eyes and gripping the arms of her chair, or the tabletop if, like now, her chair has no arms. Very much like she is a scared person waiting too long for the dentist and I am the dentist who's about to drill on her soft, rotted tooth.

All I could tell for sure was that this was bothering her.

"It's about . . . you know, guys, Ma. Just hanging around."

She shook her head. "You know how I feel about your uncle Lars, don't you, Steven?"

I certainly did.

"Well . . . no, I don't know, *exactly*, how you feel. . . ."

"Then I believe you know . . . *approximately* how I feel. I'm sorry, I truly am, for whatever went wrong in his life, and why he feels like everybody's against him. But I simply don't believe that women, and the federal government, and the Catholic church, and all minorities, and the cable company, are in cahoots to bring him down. I just don't believe it. And I don't believe apprenticing with Lars and his rootin'-tootin' buddies is going to broaden the horizons of *your* little group."

The way her voice swung upward toward the end there, it sounded like she had asked me a question. But I couldn't find one.

"What's *cahoots*, Ma?" I had never heard the word before, except possibly from Yosemite Sam. I'd certainly never heard it out of Lars.

Ma rested her chin on the table. Sighed. "Conspiracy. It means conspiracy."

Oh yessss. I do believe I'd heard *that* word before. And I do believe I'd heard it out of old Uncle Lars a time or two . . . thousand.

"Listen, Ma," I said, reaching out to brush her cheek as it rested there on the Formica. I really did like her a lot, and I wanted her to feel better. "All of that, it has nothing to do with me. We guys, my guys, we're just getting together at a place where guys can be guys. Where nobody can tell nobody what to do—except for me; I tell *everybody* what to do. It's just a Johnny—"

"Don't say it!" Ma spewed, pulling away from me.

"What? It's a Johnny Chesthair kind of a club, that's all."

"Ahhhh," she kind of screamed, but not really *scream*-screamed. "My god, not another one, please, not another one?"

All I could do, really, was sit there and watch her. And eat my eggs. But the toast was stone-cold by now, though, so nothing doing with the runny eggs and no toast.

"Think maybe you're taking all this a little too seriously there, Ma?" I got up from the table, and was careful to use my napkin—again, something I do because I know it makes her happy.

"Steven," she said, rising to see me to the door. She was still way taller than me, but I was working on it. She looked around before saying more, as if the joint was bugged. "I am *so* worried," she whispered, "that you're going to turn out just like him."

I put both hands on her shoulders and squeezed, to make her feel secure. "Ma, Lars and me are nothing alike, and we won't ever be."

"I meant your father," she said.

"*Ma,*" I gasped, but I laughed too.

"If you tell him, I'll deny it. I'll deny I ever said it. It'll be my word against yours, and he's known me a lot longer. . . . None of this was anybody's fault. I was very young when we got married. How was he to know I was still growing? There's no shame in a woman being taller than a man, everyone has told him that, but it's no use. . . ."

She's not *that* much taller than him anyway.

Later, back at the He-Man ranch, I felt a powerful urge to do some rule-making.

"I'm making some new rules," I said to Jerome and Wolfbang. Wolf was busy noodling around under the hood of the Lincoln, his body draped over the fender while his head and arms were swallowed up inside. Jerome, on the other hand, was paying me close attention as we sat in the front seat. Ling was late.

"Wolf," I yelled. "You hear me?" I blew the horn.

"Yaaaaaaaaaa!" he wailed. I could see into the thin space just above the dashboard but beneath the open hood, as he dragged himself across the engine compartment and disconnected the battery. "There, *Officer Stevie,* your power's been shut off."

"No it hasn't," I insisted. He ignored me and went back to work. "First," I announced, "everyone is required to grow a mustache."

Wolf laughed hysterically, but kept on working.

"Because I said so," I said. Habit, I guess.

"I didn't ask why," Jerome said. "How long do we get to grow this mustache?"

"ASAP. We need to get our image hardened up. How often do you shave?"

"Summer or winter?"

"Huh? Jerome, what difference does that make?"

"It's a fact; a guy's hairs grow stronger in the summer."

"Okay. Winter. How often do you shave in winter?"

"Never."

"Summer?"

"Once."

"Once? Once what, Jerome? Once a week, once a month?"

"Once. Once last year, in summer. I found a hair. I shaved it. I've been fine since. It wasn't a mustache hair, though. It was way over here. . . ."

He was trying to show me, but I was too disgusted even to look. I got out of the car and went up to see what Wolf was doing.

"What is that?" I asked him as he hung there with some greasy hunk of engine in his hands like a doctor delivering a new baby.

"It's the starter. I removed it all by myself."

"Terrific, Wolf," I said, as sarcastically as I could, which was a waste of time. Wolf was totally sarcasm-proof. "I thought the car had a fuel pump problem. Was there something wrong with the starter?"

He shrugged; he smiled.

"Isn't the idea to *fix* the car, rather than break it?"

He shrugged; he smiled. Wolf, for one, was getting his full money's worth out of this club.

"Wolfbang, you do know whose car this is, don't you?"

"That would be . . . *your* car, right, General?"

The way he said it, the conversation was over. He was only going to get worse, because he was having too much fun.

"Just *put* that back in the car," I barked.

"Yes, Captain," he answered. Which would have been great, but he didn't really mean it.

I walked back to where Jerome was sitting in the car. I peeked in.

"My mom wants to come down and see the club," he blurted.

"What!" I shrieked so loud that Lars screamed back at me from the far end of the garage.

"I mean it!" Lars said. He didn't have to specify. He'd been threatening to evict us since Jerome drew a full set of clothes on each and every month of his calendar girls. Very nice outfits, though.

104

"She doesn't want to stay long or anything. Just, you know, drop by, check out the facilities, maybe bring us a snack . . ."

It was, without a doubt, time to make a stand. I couldn't remember if I had made a stand in the last hour or so, but this definitely rated a stand. I climbed up on the roof of the car, felt it wah-wah under the weight of me, and I let him have it.

"No! No! No! No! Jerome, holy smokes, if we stand for one thing here, it's got to be *No Mothers*. This is *not* a mothers kind of a club. It's a—"

I stopped in midsentence when Jerome covered his ears with both hands and Wolfbang started simultaneously screaming as loud as he could.

"*He-Man*, remember, guys? H-E M-A-N. Secret society, special place, exclusive. No girls. No non-members. Above all, no mothers, since they fall into *every* forbidden category, for crying out loud."

Then the door opened at the back of the garage and last-of-winter afternoon light poured in, blinding us for a moment if we looked straight into it. "And *you*," I screamed toward Ling as I hopped up and down on the car roof for added power and intimidation. I saw my badge glimmer from my chest, and felt my authority surge. "We have rules here, and if you can't even get yourself here on time . . . and I don't even care if you cry your eyeballs out, I'm telling you . . ."

The door closed, my sight returned, and my throat went bone dry. It was not Ling-Ling.

It was my mother.

"What?" Jerome asked after I slid like a raindrop from the top of the car to the garage floor. "What, Steven? Who is *she*?"

That was right. None of the guys had ever met her. She could be anybody. Perhaps there was a chance of escape.

"Come on, get your coats, get your coats. We're going for a walk," I said as Ma disappeared into Lars's office.

"Sorry," Wolf said. "I don't do walks."

"Then do whatever you do, but let's go. I'm the boss—"

I had my jacket on and was already sweating, flapping my arms and tossing orders in every direction.

"Well, I feel better already," my mom said, putting her hands on my shoulders. I jumped like a cat.

"What are you *doing* here . . . lady?" I growled.

"I came to check out your club . . . boy," she answered.

"I *heard* that, Wolfbang," I called, even though he hadn't said a thing.

"And I thought you boys could use a snack," Mom said.

Wolf was off the car, into the chair, and motoring toward us faster than an Indy 500 tire change. "Foooood. Yee-hah. Thank you, lady, whoever you are."

"Ahhhhh," Jerome deduced. "Your *mom*. I thought we had a strict rule against—"

"Shut up. She's not my mother."

"Steven!" my mother gasped. Not the mock gasp like when my father says something dirty, but the real, gaspy gasp. Mothers get all bent out of shape, I guess, when you say they're not your mother.

"Ma," I said. "What are you doing to me here? You're killing me in front of my boys. *Killing* me."

"Sorry, son. I didn't mean to be killing you."

"No, don't kill him, ma'am," Wolf said as he wolfed a thick tuna sandwich. "Don't kill him, 'cause we can't be left without our fearless leader."

Ma looked down at me with new pride. "That is so nice," she said. "That is such a great thing for a mother to hear. I guess you are doing pretty well with this, then. They respect you."

This just made it more embarrassing. "He was being sarcastic, Mom. Wolf doesn't say nice things about anybody unless he's lying. That's how he gets his kicks."

"Is that true?" she asked Wolf directly.

"Not at all," Wolf answered. "But what is true is that this tuna sandwich isn't too watery at all, and that's a great hat you have on."

I walked right over and slugged him in the chest. "That's my *mother,* you animal."

"Well, at least you're acknowledging me now," she said. She still looked a little confused. "But I can see you guys want some space, so I'll just get on out of your way now." As the other guys dug through the huge bag of sandwiches and cookies, she called me over and whispered, "I suppose this isn't so bad, since you and your friends play way down here and Lars and his friends play way up there. And it's very nice that he's put clothes on his calendar this year. That's a good sign."

I just nodded, and smiled. She turned to go, and walked right into Ling-Ling, who was just as tall as she was.

"Oh dear." There was that gasp again. But this time, we all did it. Because this version of member Ling-Ling—who was an eyeful to begin with—was surely gasp-inducing. He had already slipped out of his jacket, revealing the getup underneath: olive green army pants; tight camouflage T-shirt that revealed every one of his bumps and rolls and squishies that we all could have lived without seeing; black sweatbands that were so wide they ran from his wrists all the way up over his elbows. He had a fanny pack strapped around his whole lotta waist, and when he moved, something inside jingled. Something inside the pack, that is.

"I'm his mother," Ma muttered in an apparent attempt to defend herself.

"Acknowledged," Ling acknowledged.

"What is this?" I asked, pointing at . . . all of him.

"It's gear," he said flatly.

"Yo, Ling," Wolf called. "Want a sandwich?"

Ling-Ling held up both hands in front of his face. "No. I never eat in front of people. Never eat within range of others who are eating. Never eat out of community food sources."

"You took a whole clawful of Chips Ahoys out of my bag last week," Jerome protested.

"That was before," said Ling.

I noticed that Ling-Ling's usual stack of magazines was about twice as thick as it used to be. And that now he carried *both* kinds.

My mother slipped quietly, rapidly away.

"So, then," Jerome said as soon as she was gone. "When can we book *my* mother?"

I ignored him to concentrate on Ling. "How come you're late?" I asked.

"Did some visiting," he answered, taking his usual seat in the back of my Lincoln. He spread out his magazines across the backseat. There were at least as many *American Survival Guide*s as *Wolverine*s.

"Visiting the other club, right?"

"Oooohh," Wolf called, now eating and working on the car at the same time. Filthy. "He's getting jealous now, Ling. Don't get Steven all feisty there. He's got a wicked jealousy thing going on these days."

"Ya, I was at the other club. They're pretty interesting guys."

"Ya," Jerome said. "They're interesting. Kind of like death row is interesting."

Ling was unfazed. "Boss, can we get a TV in here? I think we're missing out on a lot of important stuff in the world when we're sitting around all the time doing nothing."

There were several elements in that question which I probably should have addressed. There was only one that really stuck, though.

Boss. Boss? What an excellent club member Ling-Ling was blossoming into.

"Sure," I said. "If you can find a TV, we can have one."

Ling went back to the front of the garage, lifted his jacket from where he'd left it in a heap, and pulled out a cube with a handle. As he walked back our way, it became apparent it was a TV. The TV we'd seen at the nutso club.

"They got a new one, so they said we could have theirs. Cool, huh? They're kind of like our sponsors."

"Ya, that's cool," Jerome said. "Hurry up and turn it on so we can watch our *sponsors* on *America's Most Wanted*."

Ling-Ling had hooked up the TV and was finagling a station. "Look, I got her, I got her," he said, all excited. He'd located the talk show Boo and company had been watching the other day, the *Wendy Wightman Show*.

I shrugged at Wolf, who shrugged at Jerome, who shrugged at me. We picked up the bag of snacks and hunkered down by the TV, all of us flopping in or on the car.

Our car.

Lying there, we were finally coming together as a team. Awesome.

"Anyhow," Ling slipped in, cool as could be,

"we needed a TV here so we could all be together when we watch ourselves on *that*." He pointed. At the program.

"When we're on *that*, Ling?" I asked. "What that?"

Ever see a panda grin? Neither had I. Till now.

"*That* that," he said. "We're going on the *Wendy Wightman Show*."

12
All the Rage

How it happened was, Ling's buddies over at Patriot Central answered one of those on-screen ads. You know, during the commercial break while the People Who Married Their Pets or Survivors of Childhood Male-Pattern Baldness rest their tired lungs, where they flash the info up at the home audience to invite guests on future shows. *If you have had four or more organs removed and would like to be on our show . . . If you weigh more than your car . . . If you have been buried alive more than once . . .*

But we were going on for a much more normal reason. We were going on the show they were calling "The Men's Movement, and the State of American Manhood."

Sounds about right, doesn't it?

Boo and his Captains America Club had answered the ad a couple of months back, and when

Wendy's people called to give them the green light, he pitched them *us* as the future of the movement.

Sounds about right, doesn't it?

They interviewed He-Man Ling-Ling and were reportedly much impressed.

Now, does that sound right to you? Me neither. No matter. We were going on the Box.

We sat in the green room—where all the celebs hang out before the show—which was not green at all, but a creamy peach color. "They say that's the best color to keep our guests calm and nonviolent before they go on," explained the girl who led us to the room. "But usually it doesn't seem to work."

We were there with Boo and Kevin from the Captains America, and Leon and Zeke from some group called Rebel Yell. The Rebs looked an awful lot like fat bearded Hell's Angels, but they did wear patches on their jackets that said they were not. And they wore ties.

Ling-Ling was the one guy in the room who looked like he could have belonged to all of the clubs. He was in full nut-boy gear—black beret, dark sunglasses, fingerless leather gloves, baggy fatigues tucked into high black boots. Ling was ready for showtime.

A long buffet table was laid with potato salad and chicken wings and lasagna and fruit and chocolate-chocolate-chip cookies. Wolf, Boo, and both Rebels spent the entire half-hour preshow chomping at the buffet. Ling paced and looked suspiciously at the food. I paced. Jerome curled up in a chair, hugged his knees to his chest, and trembled.

"You sick?" I asked Jerome. No response. "You should go home then."

"No way."

"You look like death. Probably you'll look even worse on TV. Go home."

Jerome unclutched one bony little hand from one bony little leg. Pointed a crooked little finger at me. "I hope I *do* look like death. Maybe that will look tough on TV. As long as I don't look like squirrely little Jerome, that's all that matters. I told everyone in the entire world about this. I told my mother. I told my brother, who I don't tell *anything*. I told my father, who went out and bought six cases of beer and invited all six of his friends over and took the day off to watch this, like it was the *Apollo 13* moon launch. I told every single kid in every single class in school. I posted fliers. Steven, I am going on TV as the future of manhood in America! Do you have any idea how often I get called something like that?"

"I can probably guess," I said.

"Exactly," he said. "Which is why I'm going out on that set even if I puke my guts out for the crowd, even if going on that set is the very thing that is *making* me sick!"

There really wasn't much to say to that. But as group leader, I figured I should try. "Piece of fruit, Jerome? I think maybe a piece of fruit will help you feel better."

He gagged. He retched. He recovered. He shook his head and waved me away.

"Two minutes," Ted, the assistant director, called from the doorway.

"Hey *you*!" yelled one of the Rebel Yells. "Where's the security?"

"Excuse me?" Ted asked.

"The security. They made us give up our weapons at the door, and they swore there would be heavy security to compensate."

"Well, you can relax. This is a very safe and secure building. As you could see when they disarmed you."

"Not good enough," Leon snarled.

Ted had apparently been snarled at by worse than Leon. "It's going to have to be good enough," he said, smiling.

Leon looked at Zeke, who mumbled something and gestured at—gulp—me.

"Ya," Leon said. "Good point. Why are we out-numbered? We were told we were only allowed to bring along two members, and they got four. We don't like this sneaky stuff, not one bit."

Ted looked at me and my crew. "Them? You're afraid of being outnumbered by *them*?"

Ted laughed in their faces. I myself didn't see what was so funny. Wolf did, and laughed along.

"Get a load of yourselves, ya big babies," Ted taunted. "As a matter of fact, they were supposed to bring only two, but so what. They're so . . . little. Who's even going to notice?"

"So, we want them cleared out of the building, right now," Zeke insisted.

"Shut up," Ted said. "You two are up first, so you better pull yourselves together."

"Or pull *you* apart," Zeke growled.

"Boohoo," Ted said, checking things off on his clipboard, checking the buffet, taking a sip from his bottled water. "This week you're going to kill me. Last week it was the Nazis, the week before it was the National Organization of Pro-Life Women Priests. How dead can I get?"

The Rebel Yells were getting awfully frustrated trying to bully Ted. They regrouped, huddled.

"Then we quit," Zeke said mightily. "We're out of here."

"Okeydokey smokey," Ted said. "Captains America, please follow me."

They followed, marching like out-of-shape tin soldiers. Boo turned to Ling and gave him a salute. And a wink. Nice touch, Boo.

There was a big monitor up on the wall over the food, and as the show started, the fiery theme music and Wendy Wightman's perfect porcelain face came into our little lives there in the green room.

And then there they were, the Captains America.

"I think I'm going to be sick," Jerome said in that unmistakable voice that bubbles up just before a person upchucks.

"Don't," I commanded as I watched. I stood far back from the screen, but Ling-Ling and Wolfbang were pulled toward it like madmen are to the moon.

"Today's surging men's movement." Wendy announced. *"These men-only social clubs appear to be all the rage. They call themselves Real Men. They call themselves Promise Keepers. They call themselves patriots and survivalists and separatists and they call themselves He-Men."*

Wendy had a great voice. No wonder she was on TV. She made us sound so . . . grand, so mighty, so significant.

"They're so big," she continued, and the crowd started egging her on. *"They're so strong. They're so*

smart and determined and united and . . . *THEY'RE SO AFRAID!*"

The crowd went nuts. Screaming, like Elvis—the skinny Elvis from the fifties—had just walked in. And just like for him, this crowd sounded awfully high-pitched.

"Oh no," I said.

"*What are they so afraid of?*" Wendy screeched on in that awful voice of hers. "*Why do they need to cluster like packs of craven hyenas?*"

"Why?" the voices screamed back, like this was some kind of gospel show. "Why, Wendy, why?"

Wendy turned her back on the Captains America guys—who were squirming in their chairs as if they had forgotten to make a stop at the bathroom—and faced her audience.

"*Because you, sisters, are their biggest nightmare!*" she screamed. They screamed.

"Holy smokes," I said. "Lookit!"

Every last audience member was a woman.

"I can't hold it anymore!" Jerome wailed, running out of the green room in search of a safe bathroom.

"I'm going with you!" I said, chasing close behind.

Wolfbang was laughing and eating when we left, and he was still laughing and eating when we returned, just in time to see Boo and Kevin exit the stage to a symphony of hisses and, well, boos.

"Thank you, you're too kind," Boo said, acknowledging the boos.

Wolf laughed and applauded.

"You think this is *funny*?" I asked.

"Sure," Wolf said. "Lighten up. What's the worst they could do to us?"

That seemed to strike a chord for Jerome. "Oh my god," he gasped.

"Jerome?" Wolf asked. "You going to make it?"

He nodded a none-too-hearty nod.

"You don't have to go through with it," Wolf said, wheeling up close to where Jerome was slumping. "You can stay here. We'll carry it for you. I'll wave to your mom and stuff. It's not like I'll be tied up waving to my own mother, wherever the rotten old—"

"No, thanks. I'm going on," Jerome said. If nothing else came of this, Jerome was showing us all a layer of leather we knew nothing about.

I looked up at the screen, where somebody was hurling a fat black shoe at one of the empty chairs where we'd soon be sitting.

"See, look at that," I said. "I knew this had the potential for violence."

"They're only girls," Ling-Ling said.

"Ya," Wolf added. "Let 'em get violent. That could be fun."

"I say we run," I said. "How do we get out of here before they come after us?"

"Steven, Steven, Steven," Wolf said, his voice fat with disapproval and disgust. "I'm very surprised at what I'm seeing here."

Ling-Ling's look, as he turned from the screen and toward me, echoed what Wolf had just said.

"I'm only thinking of my men," I said, putting an arm around the withering shoulders of Jerome.

"Time, kiddies," Ted called, and even I was impressed with what happened then.

The three of them—Wolf, Ling, and even Jerome—straightened up and turned toward the door in one seamless, coordinated motion, like the Dallas Cowboys' offensive line just before the snap. And, led by Ling, they filed out, the squeak of Wolf's tires on the linoleum the only sound.

"You don't have to come if you don't want to, Steven," Jerome said from the rear, shaming me into action.

It was deafening.

The sound of whistles, moans, shrieks, giggles,

and war whoops as we filed across to our positions on stage.

"Aren't they just . . . adorable," our hostess said with mock surprise. "Couldn't you just pick 'em right up and squeeeeeze them?"

Oh, I see your little game. Make us look dinky.

"Since we've only got a few minutes, boys, let's get right down to it, shall we? Ahhh . . ." Wendy riffled through her index cards. ". . . Steven. You're the leader here, I understand."

Is it that obvious? I blushed, but figured the makeup covered it. I sat up straight. "That's right, ma'am."

Why all the giggling at the word *ma'am*?

"Do you hate your mother, Steven? Is that where all this malarkey comes from? What did your mother do to you to make you this way?"

I heard a gasp come out of me—amplified—that sounded like somebody opening a can of Coke fifty million gallons large.

"M-m-m-m-m-my . . . m-m-m-moth—"

"Oh, you poor thing," she said. "You can't even talk about it, can you?"

I managed to make it worse.

"N-n-n-no," I said. "I c-can't."

Brilliant, Steve-o. There's leadership for you,

ladies and gentlemen. There's backbone.

"Let me move on, then. Which one is Ling-Ling? Oh . . . oh my goodness . . . yes, of course you are. Well, they tell me, Mr. Ling, that you are the club's rough-and-ready, hell-bent-for-leather, life-size action figure. Tell me, where on earth does a boy your age get all the rage necessary to . . ."

I should stop here to comment that, while Wendy Wightman had seen just about everything over the years her sleazeball tabloid creepshow had been on TV—not that it was a *bad* show, mind you—the He-Man Women Haters Club seemed to have her thrown for a good long loop.

Because when Ling-Ling started crying, those patented Panda tears blobbing out from behind his cool shades . . .

"Oh, my dear . . . what have I done . . . you poor thing. . . ."

And Wendy "The Whip" Wightman, for the first time on TV—probably for the first time in her wicked rotten life—raced up and embraced another human being. Her arms fully extended to reach around Ling's head, she let out a groan of pity, rubbed his neck, and made a there-there clicking sound with her tongue. For his part, Ling went right with it, leaning into her, removing his beret and burying his face in her padded shoulder.

I felt my lips moving as I prayed, really prayed, and—Yes!—the closing theme music started playing. Sweat, mixed with makeup, coated my face like cellophane.

Jerome was a rock. Literally. He was so petrified he didn't even blink. He kept making that alarming throat noise, though, the kind of small swallow thing you do when you're fighting to keep something down.

Wolf didn't care that he wasn't being asked any questions. He waved at the cameras, and blurted out, "Hi, mom . . . you rotten old . . ." just like he'd practiced.

While still comforting Ling, rocking him back and forth like the *Guinness Book* world's most enormous baby, Wendy said to the audience, "We have time for maybe one question, if there's anything—"

Jerome made the swallow noise again. I didn't think he was going to pull through. He made it again. It was getting louder, right in my ear he was doing it.

"Okay . . . yes, you, there, in the Girl Scout uniform."

Do not adjust your sets. Yes, you heard correctly.

"Hey, hey, cookie girl," Wolf said.

Aaaaaaahhhhhhhhhhhhh!

Jerome gulped. He gulped. The gulping went out over the sound system.

The cookie girl pointed at me. "I have a question for Johnny Ches—"

"*Time out!*" I yelled, like a fool, jumping out of my chair, making the referee's *T* sign with my hands. "Excuse me, Wendy, but can we have some rules, here? . . . Aren't there some kind of rules for, like, you know, *who* gets to ask a question, and *what* that question might be? Perhaps we could have the questions submitted in writing, and my associates and I could consider them. . . ."

The tittering was rampant throughout the audience. Monica tittered most thunderously, since she was holding the microphone.

"*Rules?*" Wendy asked thoughtfully, stroking her chin. At least she appeared to be giving it serious consideration.

"*No!*" she answered with a vile smile.

"See, I knew it," I said, as a couple of Wendy's goons helped me back down into my seat. "No rules. Not for the girls, no sirreee. There are no rules at all for girls. They just go around doing whatever they . . . I knew it. See, *she* even gets to stand . . . how come I have to sit down?"

125

"*Go on, young lady,*" Wendy said to Monica.

"Thank you," Monica said sweetly. "I just wanted to ask Johnny Chesthair"—she could barely be heard over the roar now—"if the reason he hates girls is because I beat him up . . ."

The room began to swim. All those girls in the audience, swimming around my sweaty head like we were in a great big aquarium. Jerome's froglike gulping grew louder.

". . . and if I could cure him by taking him out for a sundae after the show?"

When her question finally ended, I responded.

I threw up, a geyser, all over myself.

13
The Coup

They sent us a copy of the tape. Thanks, Wendy.

But we decided to wait. As a group, we decided.

That was the good thing that came out of our television disaster—we started making decisions together. We decided to decide things.

First, we decided that no one club member would ever again make such a huge decision alone, such as when Ling got us on TV. This decision was unanimous.

Second, we decided we were not really a television kind of a club. If the newspapers wanted to talk to us, that would be fine, but no more TV appearances. The vote was three to one. Wolf wanted to do it all over again.

Third, we decided we should all be together, at the clubhouse, when we watched the program. And since we didn't have a VCR, that meant waiting another week until the station actually broadcast the show.

That was not a problem. Except for Wolfbang, I don't think any of us minded not seeing the program right away. Some of us might not have minded waiting a year or three.

But we did need to see it.

Wolf brought snacks, as he'd promised. We were all sitting there already, me, Ling, and Jerome, staring at the dark screen like we were being kept after school.

"Hey, slackers," Wolf said, wheeling up at high speed. "Turn it on. It's time, it's time."

I flipped the box on while Wolf went around handing out the food—a package of raw hot dogs and a jar of radioactive red maraschino cherries. Ling declined community food, as usual. Jerome merely clutched his stomach and shook his head. Could have been the food, could have been the entertainment.

I took a dog and a fistful of cherries and braced for the worst.

Wendy came on. Foul evil ratings-queen Wendy. If America only knew her like *I* know her . . .

The Captains America came on, absorbed some abuse, dished out some abuse, but mostly, just got the show all noisy. I honestly couldn't tell what it was all about.

I had a little trouble concentrating.

The He-Man Women Haters Club paraded onstage to much jazzier music, to much wilder fan reaction, than I recalled.

"Did that really happen?" I asked.

"Sure it did," Wolf said, boogeying there in his seat. "Go boys, go," he yelled at the screen.

"It did not," Jerome said. "They added all that noise afterward."

"Ling," Wolf called as Ling leaned closer and closer to the screen. "You still with us there, boy?"

Ling sighed. His nose was practically flat to the screen as Wendy hugged the little Ling-Ling in the box. "Gimme a hot dog, wouldja?" I don't think he even chewed it.

I slapped myself in the head as I heard the part again where Wendy twisted up my whole relationship with my mother.

"Boy, are *you* going to have a long night at home," Wolf laughed.

"Pass me the cherry jar," I said.

I turned from the screen and watched Jerome watching Jerome. A small smile was slowly taking over his face as he saw this thing through.

"I'll take a hot dog now," Jerome said.

"You made it, Jerome," I said, punching the side

of his head. But not hard. The good head-punch. "You held your cookies. You did the show, you stuck it out, you made everybody watch. . . . It was like one of those Indian manhood rituals."

The smile grew broad now.

"I never thought you'd make it, Jerome," Wolf said. "Not in a million years."

"No way," Ling agreed.

And then, of course, we all watched and waited for the big finale.

". . . *time for maybe one question, if there's anything . . .*"

There she was, Monica Devil Girl, in full close-up.

"Sorry," Wolf said, "but there ain't no way I'm hating that woman."

I stood in front of the TV so he couldn't look at her anymore.

Why did I do that?

Ling shoved me aside, and as Monica's voice snaked its way out of the TV speaker and into my club, the other three He-Men sang along with her.

"Johnnn-nnnyyyy . . . Chesthairrrrrr," they howled at me.

This time, I laughed. But I also covered my face.

Then we watched, anxious, to see just *what* they

were going to show—of my little accident—and what they'd cut.

I sighed happily when they didn't show me at all. The camera stayed with Monica as she finished her question. Then it pulled back for a wide shot of the entire audience recoiling, saying *yuuuuuuuuck,* all at once.

Monica had her hands covering her mouth—just like the rest of the crowd did—as the closing credits rolled over her wicked, wicked face. Except I think *she* was laughing.

"Sure, you think it's funny *there,*" I said to the screen. "But you weren't so amused when Johnny Chest-heave came to collect his sundae, though, huh? What am I, *unattractive* when I'm covered in puke?"

Jerome stepped up and snapped off the TV. Then, as one well-drilled unit, the three of them turned to face me.

"There's one more thing, Steven," Jerome said.

"Huh?"

"We had a secret meeting yesterday, without you."

"Without *me*?" I practically fell on the floor. "A secret meeting without the leader?"

"Well, that's kind of the point," Ling said. "It

was a meeting to address our leadership problem."

"Leadership . . . no . . ." I said. "No way . . . you must be pulling my—"

"The vote was unanimous, Steven," Jerome said.

Jerome sounded awfully full of control and power all of a sudden.

"Nooooooo . . ." I said, running to take refuge behind the wheel of the Lincoln.

I slammed the door, leaned on the horn.

But the battery was disconnected.